The One Hundred

Zia Ahmad

INDUS VALLEY PRESS

Copyright © 2011 Zia Ahmad

All rights reserved.

ISBN:10 0984756108
ISBN-13:9780984756100

ACCLAIM FOR

THE ONE HUNDRED

I was fascinated by this book, not just because I know nothing about street urchins in Lahore or because I know there are horrors children everywhere have to go through and this story is not shy about laying that right out there, but because I truly cared about the characters.

This is a "pathetic" book—I mean that word in its first dictionary definition and in the original Greek-root (pathos) sense of the word: one that allows us to experience the lives of the characters, suffer with them, feel compassion toward them, and in the end, cheer for them.

— Anne-Marie Bogdan
  Former copy editor at Encyclopædia Britannica

CONTENTS

	Prologue	7
1	They Escape	10
2	Raja	39
3	Lahore	72
4	Mina	104
5	Daud	144
6	The Letter	161
7	Constantine	196
8	The Killer	207
9	The Alliance	253
10	The Break-in	275
11	Goodbye	297

To Scott, my partner, my *noor*, whose support has been monumental.

PROLOGUE

October 10, 2000

He slowly opened his eyes. A deep, sluggish breath exhaled from his mouth. The coldness of black tar paving soaked into his chest as he blinked his eyes. He wondered how he had ended up lying on his stomach in the middle of the road. He heard voices, distorted, far-flung, as if he was submerged in shallow water. The dust in front of his mouth scattered as he took another deep breath and exhaled.

With his left cheek hard-pressed against the road, he saw several boys his age, attacking four men on the ground. He tried to get up by pushing himself off the road. Shooting pain invaded his body. He realized his left eye was swollen shut, his ears were ringing and there was crusty dried blood sticking from the corner of his mouth.

He grabbed his head and tried to squeeze the numbing pain out. As he looked again at the mob in front of him, he recognized one of the men on the ground, taking punches from the gang. Among the assailants, he identified one boy, Meera. He knew Meera. His head started to spin as his blurry vision cleared and memories trickled back in. Muted voices turned into screams and shouts. In the background, the sound of crickets and other night creatures got louder, tearing through the silence of the night. He staggered back on his feet. He was remembering now. He heard his name being called:

"Yosef, hurry!"

He turned to look. And like a flash, it all came back. Yosef recalled why he was there. The pain, the swollen eye — it was as if he were waking up from a dream. His eyes roamed for his companions, Jogi and Saif. They were nowhere in sight. His heart started to beat faster. Things had not gone as planned. Yosef looked ahead at the building in front of him, the police station. He was supposed to be inside that building at this hour, not outside, he remembered.

Yosef looked over his shoulder and gave one more look at the mob calling his name before inching toward the police station. His wounded knee made each step feel like daggers falling from the sky and piercing deep into the flesh. He bit into his lips to cut the pain. There was not much time left. Having no sense of how long he had been out cold, it could now be too late. With clenched teeth and tightened muscles, he staggered forward toward the building.

Yosef passed the courtyard and entered through the main door. Hatim was slumped on the floor, unconscious. The middle drawer of his desk was half open. There was no gun attached to his holster. He looked around once again for Jogi and Saif. There were voices coming from the hall way. Someone shouted. Yosef followed the voices. He placed his hands on both walls of the narrow hall for support as he staggered down. In the third cell on the right he saw someone sitting on the floor inside, with his back pressed against the iron bars. That was Saif. His face was cupped in his hands; his shoulders jerked as he sobbed. They had made it inside the cell, Yosef thought. He then saw the man sitting on the cell's wooden bench, across from Saif, wearing a prison suit.

Half of the man's face was shadowed in the dark, but that did not stop Yosef from recognizing who he was. That man was the reason he was here. He heard the man talking to Saif. This was the moment Yosef had been waiting for. He heard the clock tick in his head.

"I pity you," Yosef heard the man say. Saif had developed hiccups in between his sobbing. Yosef looked into the man's eyes. They were cold. An icy feeling ran down Yosef's spine. It was as if he was seeing him vicariously through Daud. He wondered if Daud felt the same chill staring into the eyes of a monster. The man looked up in Yosef's direction. Their eyes met. Yosef let out a growl and entered the cell.

1 THEY ESCAPE

February 6, 1998

The bus turned a sharp corner as it cut across the steep curve on the narrow, two-way, unpaved mountain road. It shook up the passengers inside, waking some of them up. There was little lighting inside the bus, and the yellow plastic on some of the seats was torn. One could see, if one looked hard enough through the smudged windows, the deep valley down below in the black of the night, illuminated by occasional moonlight set free from stray patches of clouds. Blue light reflected on marble-white snow gathered on rocks and boulders along the road under the cold February sky. The driver was going south on a downhill slope at the very edge of the road. The far edge of the right wheel spun off the gravel road at a treacherously high velocity. One wrong turn and the bus could go tumbling down, deep into the dark abyss, into the Swat River. He seemed experienced enough, through his maneuvers. He must have driven down that route multiple times.

Unlike their fellow passengers, the two boys in the middle row were wide awake. A little shaken by the speeding vehicle and the violent jerks, with nervous looks on their faces, their inquisitive eyes gazed through the pitch black outside, trying to capture the view to add on to their adventure. They were both young, with black hair covered in dust, sleep-deprived puffed-up big brown eyes, and brown skin, cold and dry. The older boy appeared to be about seventeen. The younger of the two wore a T-shirt that had Bruce Lee's imprint on it. In a fairly crowded bus, no one seemed to have noticed or cared about those two. Oblivious to their fellow passengers, they clung to each other. The younger one looked at the other.

"Do you think they would know by now?"

"Be quiet. You will draw attention," the other leaned over and replied in a lowered voice. Bone-chilling air ran inside the bus. He wrapped a wool shawl around his companion and snuggled closer.

"I am scared."

"It wasn't easy for me either; we will be safe where we are going."

"I can't keep my hands from shaking." The younger of the two wrinkled his nose. "I wish I could make it stop."

"Close your eyes. Do not think about it."

"What if they come looking for us?"

"Dawn is approaching fast. At daybreak, you will see it is a big city we are going to. People go there and disappear." The older boy blew steamy breath into the palms of his hands and rubbed them together. "We will disappear, like everyone else."

The words seemed to have calmed the younger boy down. Daud, a ten-year-old, patted a small bag lying on his lap, rested his head against the window, and stared outside at nothing. His dreamy eyes blinked, and his mind drifted. His brain was too young, his mind too tired, to ponder over the events that had led him to this journey. This young man sitting next to him was now as much of a family as Daud could ever ask for. Daud had no choice but to trust him. After all, he had dragged Daud from the hell he thought he will never escape.

They had boarded the bus at Mingora, Swat, his home town. Wearing a *pakol* (a Pashtun hat), he remembered running along the banks of the Swat River, climbing lush, green, picturesque hilly slopes under the clear blue sky, playing hide and seek around a *stupa*, a mound-like structure holding Buddhist relics, surrounded by other ancient Buddhist ruins. At night, he watched his father water the mud floor of the veranda, evoking the musky earth smell, before going to sleep under the stars.

His chain of thoughts shifted as the bus turned another narrow bend. He remembered his father's face in the blue shadows of that one night, sitting at the edge of the bed, running his fingers through his son's hair.

"Please tell me a story, *Baba* (father)," Daud requested with dreamy eyes.

"What story should I tell today, *pari* (fairy) or prince Sheherzaad?"

"*Pari*," Daud chose.

"You are getting too old to listen to fairy tales," his father said and rubbed his eyes.

"*Baba*, why are you crying?"

"Sit up straight," his father said. "I have something important to tell you."

Then his father had told him that he, Daud, would need to leave the house to work. He blinked and simply listened.

"What is a loom factory?"

"It is where they make carpet."

Daud half listened to how his *Baba* was under the burden of borrowed money from a pawn broker to pay for Daud's sister's wedding. A high interest rate doubled the loan amount. And now Daud would also have to work as well as his father to pay off the debt. His young mind wondered who would be telling him stories there.

"When will I come back home, *Baba*?"

"In coming years you will understand, *noor* (light) of my eyes. But for now, you will have to take on your family's debt."

The bus ran over a stone, lifting the back of the bus into the air, causing all the passengers to become airborne. Some plummeted back to their seats, others fell on the floor, cursing and yelling at the driver to slow down. A howling wind chased the bus.

It had been a stifling, bright day in June 1997, Daud recalled, when his father dropped him off at the front gate of the factory outside Mingora. He tried to hide behind the corner of father's *kameez* (long tunic), which flapped with the warm, dusty breeze. But he was soon pulled out by strong hands. His father held him tight in a warm and firm hug for a while and said, "You be a good boy, my son."

Daud watched his father's scooter disappear behind a thick cloud of dust. Something inside him told him this was goodbye.

Yosef, Daud's companion on the bus, breathed heavily and shrank under the shawl. He had fallen asleep, resting his head on Daud's shoulder. Daud turned to look at him and listened to him snore. He rested his cheek on top of Yosef's head and closed his eyes.

Daud met Yosef in the veranda the very first day he was brought to the factory. The veranda opened toward the middle of the building, surrounded by arched pillars around a square hallway surrounding the veranda. All the rooms opened to the hallway, and the workers—who consisted mostly of children of Daud's age—were allowed out in the veranda for a few minutes a day during their lunch break. This was the only time they were allowed to leave their posts, along with one break to use the washroom. A full-time chef lived on the premises and cooked for the entire workforce.

Kaka, the chef, was a tall, beefy, stocky man in his late forties with button shaped eyes and a thick, salt-and-pepper moustache that overhung his upper lip. He proudly showed the scar on his head that started at the lower right temple and disappeared somewhere in the thickness of his glistening gray hair.

"Do you see this?" He would run his finger through his forehead, addressing a feeble, wide-eyed child, frightened by his looks. "This came from a bear attack. I nailed the big black *baloo* to the ground as he tried to break open my skull with his claws." Occasionally, in the evening, Kaka would gather the children in the large kitchen by the hearth and tell tales of his brave young days when he engaged in a wrestling match and would slam his opponent to the floor in forty seconds or less. Or the times when he won the village running contest, carrying two men on his shoulders. He offered them stale bread soaked in milk to keep them interested in his stories.

"You should consider finishing this piece of bread soon before they drag your ass back to work." Yosef approached Daud, standing against the wall in the veranda, which made him easy to spot in the crowd.

"I am not hungry."

"You should eat it anyway. Because sooner or later you will be famished. And it will be at a time when there will be nothing for you to eat." Yosef continued to munch on his bread, dipped in lentil curry. Out of the corners of his eyes, he glanced at Daud, who was staring at him dumbfounded.

"Just got dropped off, first day?"

Daud nodded, his eyes wide and full of apprehension.

"Scared?" Yosef stared back.

Daud nodded, tears welling up in his eyes. Two more children joined in the conversation.

"Hungry, scared, crying — sounds like my first day," one of them said.

"I told you I am not hungry," Daud snapped.

"Give me your bread, then." Yosef tried to snatch the hard, crusted flatbread from Daud's hands. "I'll eat it." Daud pulled his hands behind his back.

"You are hungry," Yosef laughed.

One of the other kids snuck behind Daud and snatched the bread.

"Give it back!" Daud yelled.

Another kid smacked the *pakol* off Daud's head and threw it in the air. Daud jumped in the air to grab it, but it was passed on to Yosef before he could get to it.

"Don't do this," Daud pleaded.

"Don't do what?"

Yosef and two others circled around Daud and tossed bread and hat to each other, while Daud, with teary eyes, tried to snatch them back.

That day Daud cried. He cried standing on the veranda, holding the piece of bread finally handed back to him. He cried when he was being trained on the loom, trying to tie knots to cotton fiber, hanging from the warp strings. He wept when the morning sun gave way to the growing shadows of dusk. His eyes watered when he tried to gulp down the soup and bread for dinner and choked. He bawled as he was ushered in to sleep on the floor of the backroom, shared by several others like him.

His cries, rather subdued by then, had turned into hiccups and sniffs, which sounded like whispered echoes at night. Someone from the other corner yelled and cursed out loud, asking Daud to shut up. Later that night, Yosef walked up to him and dropped the *pakol* next to him. Daud grabbed it and hugged it tightly.

"Everyone goes through this the first day," Yosef said as he sat next to Daud. "So your father sold you into bonded servitude, eh?"

"He had no choice."

"I am sure, I am sure. The sooner you get used to this place, the better it will be for you."

"How long have you been here?" Daud asked in a cracked voice.

"Long enough for me not to remember exactly when."

"I don't want to be here."

"No one does. You don't have much of a choice, *bacha* (kid)."

"I will run away!" Daud wiped his eyes with the back of his hand.

"Feel free to try it if you want to test the strength of the bones in your body. The factory owner will make sure you don't make another attempt by breaking few of them."

"I don't belong here."

"Like I said, no one does. It's best that you get used to it," Yosef said.

"Where is your home?" Daud asked Yosef.

. . .

The year was 1981. It was the year when Yosef opened his eyes to the world inside a prison in Mardan in the Swat valley, next to his incarcerated mother. He spent the first seven years of his life behinds barbed wires, high concrete walls, and iron-clad cell doors. As a toddler, he ran down the hallways and was picked up by other inmates and clasped. He played with toys made of mud, stone, and rocks picked up from the ground. Occasionally, prison guards ran after him, playfully, when he snuck up on them and tried to steal food from their plates. Every night he was locked back inside with his mother, where they both slept on the same bed.

Yosef's mother, Surya, had been accused of having an affair with her dead husband's brother and of stealing, so she was thrown into jail, pending a day in court. She was told by another woman not to hold her breath for swift justice, since she already had been waiting for a court date for four years.

At age seven Yosef was let out of the prison walls for the first time. He hadn't understand why his mother bathed him with special care, made him wear clean white dress, and cried while buttoning his shirt.

"Is today the festival of Eid, *amma* (mother)?" he asked.

All the female inmates, known to him as *khalas* (aunties), walked with him to the gate, while his mother sat inside her cell and wept. Outside, Yosef saw a man with a long gray beard and dark sunglasses, also garbed in crisp white dress. In one hand, he held a *tasbeeh* (rosary). He fingered the beads and mumbled something in his mouth. One of the prison guards held Yosef's hand and walked him to the man. The guard leaned over and said, "Say *salam* (hello) to Mullah Aziz, Yosef. He is here to take you with him."

"Where am I going?"

"Come closer, my son." Mullah Aziz motioned to Yosef and crouched. He held Yosef by the shoulders. "You are seven years old now. It is time for your learning to begin," Mullah Aziz said.

"My mother lives here."

Mullah Aziz slowly took his glasses off. He had pale gray eyes.

"Your mother is an impure human being, a lost soul, drowned in sin, *beta* (son). She has done her motherly duty to raise you this far. Now it is our turn to take you away from the shadows of her sins and enlighten you with the knowledge and wisdom of God, to teach you the ways of life and submission to one divine being."

"I can not leave my *amma*!" Yosef protested.

"It is for your own good, *bacha*," the guard said, as he lifted the kicking and screaming Yosef and put him in the back seat of Mullah Aziz's jeep.

Yosef was brought into a *madrasa* (seminary) to recite and memorize the Quran. His new home would save him from a life of sin, Mullah Aziz told Yosef, as he walked Yosef through a green metal gate, into a pale-yellow brick building. For the next four years, Yosef joined other students, who were also there to learn. He sat inside a blue-painted room with them on a straw mat, tattered at places, and recited. Rows of children sat on both sides of the extended low rising wooden benches used to put their books on, their bodies rocking back and forth, as they learned and practiced the verses through rote learning, hoping for the lesson to imprint on their memory. At night, Yosef sat on the floor with his fellow students in the dining area and ate *dahl* (mashed lentil) and *roti* (flatbread). In between those times, Yosef cleaned toilets, washed clothes, and — hoping to see his mother — stood by the front gate, watching children play soccer in a dusty playing field.

Yosef, from time to time per instructions from mullah Aziz, made and served tea to guests. The mullah's guests had long, dark beards and wore turbans. Automatic rifles hung from their shoulders.

"Come, come, *bacha*." Mullah Aziz brushed his beard with fingers. "Say *salam* to these fine men. They are your brothers. They were once students like you in this *madrasa*."

On a midsummer afternoon, when Yosef was eleven, a boy named Karim joined the *madrasa*. Karim met Yosef after midday prayer. He approached Yosef, who was surrounded by other students. Yosef had built a reputation of being a physically active and hot-tempered boy, admired by a small group of followers. He had once attacked another student during a cricket match and broken his nose. Another time, Mullah Aziz had to be called in the middle of the night to pry open Yosef's hands from the throat of a student who had been heard criticizing Yosef's weak learning skills.

"What is killing you from the inside, *bacha*?" Mullah Aziz had asked.

Yosef's inquiries about his mother had evolved as he grew older. Initially, he wept in front of the mullah, "I want to go back to my mother" and "I miss *amma*."

Later he asked, "Will she come for me once she gets out of prison?"

And then, as time went on, he simply wondered, "Does she still think about me?" "Does she miss me?" "Was she really a sinner?"

At those times, Mullah Aziz ran his hand over Yosef's head and said, "Raise your hands and pray she will be granted God's forgiveness."

Karim approached Yosef and nudged him on the elbow. He was a tall, portly 14-year-old with a flat nose and flared nostrils.

"*Salam*," he said.

Yosef turned to look at him and saw his beaming eyes.

"We have never met, but I know about you."

Dinner that night was *roti* and *sabzi*, mixed vegetables cooked in gravy sauce. Yosef sat at the low bench right across from Karim and watched him scoop *sabzi* with a small piece of bread.

"How do you know about me?" Yosef asked.

"What?" Karim shouted from across the table. The room was buzzing with children eating and gossiping.

"You said earlier you know about me," Yosef repeated. "How?"

"My father is a prison guard where your mother lived, and where you were born."

Yosef's heart started to beat faster. He placed the food he was about to put in his mouth back into the plate.

"You know my mother?"

"No, not me, my father does."

"Where is she?"

"Huh?"

"You said 'where she lived.' Does she not live there anymore?" Yosef felt his face turning red. Karim was the first person he had met in four years who claimed to have known his mother. His unanswered questions ran through his mind one by one.

"Do you know where my mother is?" Yosef asked again.

"I don't know."

"Was she released from prison?"

"Not sure."

"Did she try to contact me?" Questions rolled from Yosef's tongue. He glared at the rowdy student sitting next to him. "I will break your neck if you do not stop making that noise." He then turned to look at Karim.

"So your father knew my mother."

An uneasy feeling of anticipation crawled inside Yosef's skin. Karim might be his chance to reconnect with his mother, he thought. He would ask Mullah Aziz's permission to go visit her if she is still in prison. He would look for the village she might be living in, if she was released. What would he ask her when he saw her?

"Why didn't you come for me when you left prison, *amma*?" He pictured being in her arms, wetting her sleeve with tears.

"Not just your mother, my father also knew your father," Karim replied.

"My father?"

"Yes."

"My father died before *amma* went to jail." Yosef felt thorns piercing his throat. He ran his tongue over dry lips.

"Your father was a prison guard and worked in the same prison with mine." Karim wiped his lips after taking another bite.

Yosef felt the earth shaking. His body felt like it shattered into a thousand pieces and smashed on the floor.

"This room is very loud. Maybe I didn't hear you right. Can you repeat?" Yosef shouted.

Karim moved aside the plate and leaned forward.

"Your mother was a *randi*, a whore," he said. "She was—" Karim could not finish the sentence. A hot plate of *sabzi* flew from across the table and struck Karim's face. He let out a cry of agony as spiced curry went into his eyes. He tried to wipe the steamy vegetables running down his face. During the few seconds while Karim rubbed his eyes for clear view, he saw Yosef vanish from his seat across from the table and reappear, standing right next to him.

"You called my mother *randi*?"

Karim opened his mouth to say something, and instead howled like an animal being slaughtered. The knife in Yosef's hand plunged deep inside Karim's belly. He rolled in his own blood. Yosef dug the knife out and ran out of the room. He ran fast, across the field toward Mullah Aziz's quarter, cutting through the wind.

Mullah Aziz had just put the Quran down and was about ready to eat dinner when Yosef stormed in. His eyes were as red as the blood dripping from the tip of the knife blade.

"You told me my father died before *amma* went to prison," Yosef growled.

"What have you done, *bacha*?"

"Answer me!"

"What do you want to know? Whose blood did you spill?"

Yosef clutched the knife handle and moved forward.

"Who is my father?"

On a cold January morning the following year, Yosef sat at a bench outside the bus station, waiting for the bus to arrive. It had been over six months since he stabbed Karim. That day, Mullah Aziz had told him the truth about his parents. He shook his head as the mullah had described how Yosef's mother was raped in prison by a prison guard. The guard, a married man and his father, contacted Mullah Aziz to come take Yosef away when he turned seven. His mother, Mullah Aziz said, was to be tried as an adulterer in addition to her previous pending charges, since there were no witnesses to come forward and support her claim of rape.

"It was for your own good, *bacha*, that you didn't know this early on."

In the months that followed, Yosef stopped learning the Quran, broke noses, and stomped on students who quipped and pointed at him when he walked down the veranda. He got into more fights than Mullah Aziz could handle. Even when he was sent away to receive military training, Yosef was transported back to the *madrasa*. In the letter of rejection, Mullah Aziz read, Yosef was described as mentally incapable of following orders, being obedient, and submitting for a higher cause.

"You promise me," Yosef said to Mullah Aziz, as the latter came out with two steamy cups of tea and sat next to him on the bench. The bus had just pulled into the station, and passengers were slowly getting on board.

"Don't make me a sinner by asking me to promise what I may not be able to keep."

"Promise me you will send for me when you hear about my mother," Yosef said. Hot steam exhaled from his mouth.

Mullah Aziz snuggled under the shawl he had over his shoulders and looked ahead. "Digging through old wounds will not let you heal, my son."

"Yet seeing her is the only way that will bring calm in me."

Mullah Aziz kept his gaze forward and nodded. "Very well, *bacha*, let's get you on that bus to Mingora."

"And that is how I ended up here, working in this carpet factory," Yosef said to a droopy, heavy-lidded Daud.

"Did Mullah Aziz keep his promise?" Daud asked in a sleepy voice. Unconsciously he had held Yosef's hand all the while Yosef told his story.

"He did," Yosef said. "Last year he came to visit me." He slid further into the mattress and rested his back against the wall.

"What did he say?"

"My mother was released from prison, only to be taken up into the mountains and executed."

"What?!"

"The same militia men who attempted to give me military training accused my mother of adultery, dragged her up into the mountains, and executed her."

Daud's eyes were wide open now.

"They tied her hands behind her back and shot her in the head." Yosef took a deep breath. "Mullah Aziz told me."

. . .

Yosef taught Daud how to set up the loom. Patiently he showed him how to tie warp strings on to the loom. Day after day, they sat in front of rows of vertical looms, turning threads into fringes of the rugs. The weft ran horizontally, woven through delicate hands, intertwined with the warp to create the foundation of the rugs. Some weavers were skilled and some not so proficient, but they all tied wool knots to the warp threads.

Constant weaving for over twelve hours a day was a long and tedious process, sitting or stooping at the loom, breathing carpet dust. They were all trained to tie knots at a fast pace, constantly moving their fingers. Many complained of pain in the wrist at the end of the day. Many times the factory supervisor made them retie the knots if they made a mistake on patterns or design, repeating close to fifty or a hundred knots. A standard two-foot by six-foot rug had over a hundred thousand knots.

Endless hours of weaving and tying took its toll on Daud's tendons. The bones in some of his fingers twisted and would not straighten. The weavers were not allowed to stop during their shift, even to rub their hands. Noncompliance meant a lash on the back with a leather belt.

It was a hot summer day. A large fan ran full speed, but was not enough to beat the stifling heat that reflected off the window glass. The hall buzzed with voices and the wooden clucks of looms each time a weaving cycle was completed, kind of like a typewriter resetting itself at the end of each typed row. Each loom was assigned to three workers, all busy tying the knots as fast as possible. Daud sat at the far left corner with two others. Yosef had taught him a few tricks so he could slow down to rest his hands and fingers without any one noticing. A "click" sound of bone came from his hands. His right index finger became limp, and his hands stopped. The other two workers raised their eyebrows.

"What do you think you are doing?" one of them asked.

"I can't move my fingers!" Daud's voice resonated more with fear than from the pain he was enduring.

"He will make you work on knots all night if he spots you not working," the third worker whispered.

The pain became severe, and Daud grabbed his wrist with the other hand. Others around them noticed that work at the loom had stopped. Not being able to stand the pain, he got up and started crying. That was enough to cause everyone to stop working and turn to look at what was going on. Yosef saw Daud standing in the middle of room, sobbing. His pulse froze, and his heart sank. Through the corners of his eyes he could see the supervisor approaching.

His name was Akbar, a man in his late thirties, over six feet tall, with big hands and broad shoulders. He ran the carpet factory and supervised the labor. His sunburned skin glistened as beads of sweat dripped down his cheeks into his moustache.

"Come closer, *bacha*," he said in a bristly voice. "Let me see what is wrong."

"I can't move my fingers." Daud sniffed and spread his left hand out.

Akbar took Daud's fingers in his hands, pressing the tendons gently with his thumb.

"Does it hurt here?" he asked. "How about there?" Daud nodded.

"So soft and delicate." Akbar ran his fingers on Daud's hand. "It hurts all over, doesn't it, son?"

Daud wiped the tears from his eyelashes and nodded. He could not see the club Akbar was concealing behind his back. With Daud's hand held in Akbar's tight grip, the truncheon smashed against Daud's finger bones, making his body quiver in pain, shadows of disbelief spreading across his face.

"No … no!" Daud screamed, inching back, trying to free his hand from Akbar. Another blow caught the carpal of his wrist. Daud's scream crashed against the ceiling.

"Tell me, does it still hurt just as bad?" Akbar growled.

"Please don't beat me, *Sahib* (Sir) no …"

"Tell me if you will try to sneak off work again, making these excuses."

"No … no ... no …" Daud's plea had no effect. This time, Akbar took a swing and struck Daud's knees. He fell to the ground.

"Leave him alone, you *harami* (bastard)!" Akbar looked up and saw Yosef standing right across from him. For the next fifteen minutes, Akbar pounced on Yosef, kicking, punching, hitting.

That night, Daud lay unconscious in Yosef's arms, bruised from the beating, his body quivering in high fever. Yosef seemed unaware of his own wounds. His swollen eyes were open, staring at the space in front of him. He leaned over and whispered in Daud's ears, "We are not going to stay here long."

Fall arrived, and announced that winter was lurking right behind. They took out their long coats, parkas and shawls. Smoke-filled air rose from burning wood. Dried leaves crushed under their feet when they walked. Weeks had passed, and wounds had healed. Daud was able to get back on his feet. On his very first day back to work, his ankle was chained to the loom by Akbar.

"Any more funny business from you, and you will be back to bed. This time, I will not show any mercy." He waved his fist at Daud's face. Yosef watched from a distance, but kept quiet. He kept a close eye on Daud. Surprisingly, Akbar did not come after him for trying to rescue Daud from punishment.

In late November, the students were glued to the window and witnessed the first snowfall of the season. Wet, heavy snow fell from the sky, covering everything in white, including the power lines, causing blackout. Some cheered in glee and ran out into the veranda to play in the snow. Daud covered himself in a shawl and sat by the fireplace. He was eating *chana* (chickpea curry) and rice when Yosef came up to him and sat down.

"It is all white outside," Yosef said.

"Yes, I saw it through the window."

"How is dinner?"

Daud shrugged his shoulders.

"I want to give you an update." Lately, Yosef had been talking about his plan to escape. At night, when everyone was asleep, he whispered in Daud's ears how he was working to get them out. Daud listened.

"I heard back from my contact at the city today," Yosef mumbled in a low voice, pretending to be chewing his food. "It won't be long before we will be able to leave."

"Where will we go?" Daud asked.

"I will tell you all about it, soon. Just remember, we won't be staying here too long."

Daud, though doubtful, had seen Yosef talking to strangers at the gate when Akbar was away. Daud could not tell anything from Yosef's hand gestures. But through his cautiously roaming eyes, Daud could tell Yosef was plotting something.

Winter tightened its hold. It was an icy-cold night in February. The air was dry and silent; the sky above was clear. An occasional puttering sound of motorcycle or rickshaw shattered the stillness of the night, causing some to flinch and twist in their sleep before drifting back into it. Daud lay on a thin mattress on the floor, covered with a blanket, fast asleep amid other coworkers in the room. His wounds were now faded scars of the past.

His eyes slowly opened. Someone was shaking his shoulder. His mind slowly phased out of the haze of deep sleep. A shadow was crouched on his left side and was violently shaking him. Daud rubbed his eyes. It was Yosef.

"What are you doing?" Daud asked in a groggy voice.

"Wake up! Its time," Yosef replied.

"Time for what?"

"Time for us to leave this place."

"Tonight, now?"

"Yes, now."

"But you didn't say anything before."

"Tonight is our chance, and we are taking it."

"What are you talking about?"

"Everything is in place. I have what I need to get us out of here. You want me to sit here and tell you a story, or you want to get up and follow me?" Yosef's voice was slightly above a whisper. "I promised to get you out of this hell. Tonight is the night I deliver on my promise."

Akbar was sleeping in a room on the east side of the courtyard where the chef usually slept. Once a month, he allowed the chef—who also acted as a guard at night—to go home for two days. During those nights while the chef was gone, Akbar guarded the factory and stayed overnight.

It was the middle of the night when Akbar woke himself up from his snoring. In the dark, he noticed two shadows standing right by his bed as he turned to his side to go back to sleep.

"Who's there?" he said in a loud voice and tried to get up. To his surprise, his hands and feet were tied to the edge of the *charpoy*, a woven daybed consisting of a wooden frame strung with knotted ropes, by a rope.

"Untie me at once or I will shred every inch of flesh from your bodies," Akbar growled.

Yosef leaned over, his eyes cold and drained of any emotions. "What you should be wondering is what is going to happen to you in the next few minutes." He circled around the *charpoy* and made sure all the knots were tied securely.

"You untie me, and I may just let you live," Akbar grunted and jerked around, trying to set himself free.

"Did you think beating up a little kid like a stuffed doll will make you bigger man?" Before Akbar could reply, Yosef taped his mouth shut with duct tape. "Did you think I will forget?" Akbar's neck veins became visible; his face turned red as he grunted.

"Ever heard a story of elephants and ants?" Yosef continued on, his voice calm and cold. "The proud elephant stomped on ants, thinking he was strong and mighty. Until one night, while he was asleep, ants crawled in through his trunk, into his brain, and killed him." Akbar desperately tried to set himself free, his eyes widening in amazement and disbelief.

"Now I want you to remember this time, this day, this night when I will break your legs." From behind his arm, Yosef took out a hammer. "Before I leave, I want to make sure you never walk proud, pretending to be strong and mighty." Yosef reached under and took out a brown leather case. He handed it to Daud.

"Take this and wait for me outside," Yosef addressed Daud. Daud looked into Yosef's eyes reluctantly, as if to say something, but silently obliged and walked toward the door. He had questions, but he dared not ask them at that time.

Yosef placed a foot-long piece of lumber between Akbar's ankles. Akbar shook his head, mumbling for Yosef to stop.

"I am sorry. I cannot understand what you are saying." Yosef raised the hammer and struck the calf bone. With a loud, shattering sound, Akbar's left foot turned crooked and went limp. He shook violently on the bed and screamed in pain in a subdued voice. Next, Yosef aimed for the bottom of his right foot and struck the heel. A cracking sound was heard and Akbar's lower leg bone drove upward right through his skin, breaking out just below the kneecap. Akbar slammed his head in spasm. Intense pain made him half unconscious.

Seconds later, his body fluttered, as agonizing pain returned. Yosef stood for a minute and watched before turning to leave. He then looked over his shoulder and took another look at Akbar lying in bed, again unconscious, his broken bones beyond the point of any repair, and walked out.

"Let's go!" Yosef said to Daud, standing outside the door.

"What did you do?"

"He broke your fingers and hands. I made sure he got what he deserved."

"What about the others?" Daud asked. He trembled when he spoke.

"There is only time and energy to save two of us." Yosef paused for a moment and looked into Daud's terrified eyes. "They can find their way out if they want to. The gate will be open."

"How are we going to unlock the gate?" Daud, full of questions, barely paused between breaths.

Yosef took out a key. "All I had to do was to get a cast of the key on soap, hand that bar of soap to a friend outside, and he got me a duplicate."

"Can we go home, too?"

"Not a chance," replied Yosef. "Kaka will be back in the morning to find Akbar. They will be looking for us like hungry jackals. And the first place they will look for you will be your parent's house. I have made arrangements for us, and we are going to the city. That will be our home now."

They both walked to the bus station in the dark of the night, said a final goodbye to their home town, and boarded the first bus leaving for Lahore.

2 RAJA

August 20, 1999

"Name?"

"What?"

"Everybody has a name; do you have one?"

"Raja."

"How old are you?"

"Where is my brother?"

"I don't know where your brother is. Are you worried?"

Silence followed.

"Something is bothering you?"

"I have a headache."

"Here is a glass of water. Drink it; it will make you feel better."

"What is it?"

"Just water, cold and refreshing. So, how old are you?"

"Twelve."

"What part of town are you from, Raja?"

The sound of thunder interrupted the conversation. Lightening struck outside and illuminated the room. It was a large room with very little furniture. There was a *charpoy*, a chair, a side table, and two large metal containers placed against the left wall. The air inside the room was stale and had a rancid butcher-shop smell. There were no windows inside the room. The only natural light came from the transom, high above the door on the right wall, fenced off with vertical wrought iron bars. A dust-covered pendant, the only lighting fixture in the room, dangled from the ceiling.

There was little visibility inside the room, and the corners at the far ends were dark. Dry plaster was cracked, and it peeled off the right wall, which may have been painted white at one time. It was hard to distinguish in dim light, but there appeared to be brown spots speckled all across the left wall. If one didn't know better, it could have been mistaken for a piece of abstract art, an artist's creative imagination becoming reality by spattering the paint off the brush on to a large canvas.

A man who appeared to be in his mid-forties sat on the chair, right across from the *charpoy*. His deep-set black eyes looked intently through the large, square-frame glasses he wore. He had square cheeks, strands of white hair on the front and in his sideburns, and a thick upper lip right below the bushy moustache. He ran his fingers through neatly combed hair, parted on the left. His left cheek was raised higher than the right, giving the impression of a permanent mild smile on the face. The man seemed focused and calm. He took notes as he spoke to the boy. His eyes were fixated on Raja throughout the conversation.

"Where do you live?" The man rephrased the question.

"Green Town," Raja replied.

Raja, the twelve-year-old boy, sat on the *charpoy* across from the man. His legs were above the ground, crossed at the ankles. His sparkling hazel-brown eyes roamed around the room nervously. He wore an oversized gray sweatshirt, partially tattered on one side and imprinted with a college logo, black pants, and an old dusty hat. His fingers constantly played with the choker at his neck. On his left hand he wore a silver-wire bracelet with black beads on it. With a wheat-toned complexion, beak-shaped nose, and strong shoulders, he appeared to have worked in hard labor.

"That is a nice bracelet." The man pointed at Raja's hand.

"My brother gave it to me." There was a sense of pride in his response.

"He must be good to you. Are you a good little brother?"

"I am. We stay close," Raja replied.

A nauseated feeling churned inside Raja's stomach. He took another sip of water from the glass given to him by the man. His eyelids felt heavy, and he found it difficult to sit straight. Drops of sweat appeared on his forehead as the humidity inside the room crept up. It made his skin look shiny.

"Green Town is on the other side of the river. You are a long way from home. How many people know you are here?"

"Only my brother does."

"Do your parents know where you are?" the man asked.

"No, they don't," replied Raja.

"Maybe we should talk about it."

"You ask a lot of questions," Raja said, irritated.

"Yes, I do." The man's voice remained calm.

"Why?"

"That is the only way one can get to know another better."

"I ran away from home. I live on the streets," Raja replied after a pause.

"I know where you live."

"Why are you interested in knowing a street urchin, a *harami*?"

"No one in this room called you a *harami*."

"That's what they called me, before I ran off."

"How long has it been since you left home?"

"I don't remember; many years, I guess."

An almost unnoticeable smile slithered across the man's face.

"Tell me more," the man asked.

"Am I going to get paid for this?" Raja asked.

"Yes, you will. Just be a little patient."

"What else do you want to know, *sahib*?" Raja asked, as he took off the hat and wiped his forehead with his sleeves.

"Tell me about your family: mother?"

"One."

The man smiled at the answer.

"No father," Raja continued, without noticing the grin. "There is another man who lives in the house now; calls himself my father but he is not."

"Do you like him?" the man asked.

"Shit, that *harami*!" Raja's face turned red as he snickered.

"You have some tongue on you for a twelve-year old," the man said.

"What's it to you?" Raja snapped.

"Tell me about the man who lives in your house now."

"He is a bum and a drunk. He comes home at night, stinking of *sharaab* (alcohol). He beats my mother with whatever he gets his hands on if she didn't cook the food to his taste. He pinned me and *bhai* (brother) to the ground, punched us, and took all the money we made, called my mom *randi*. Ask me again if I like him."

"I can tell that it made you angry," the man said.

"What would you have done if you were me?" Raja bellowed. "I wanted to crack open his skull each time he laid his hands on me."

"Did you ever stand up against him?"

"I could not. He was too strong even when drunk." There was a hint of defeat in Raja's resentment.

"Did you feel weak against him, helpless, reversing your anger inside you?"

Raja did not say anything in response.

"So nobody came to rescue you from your stepfather?"

"He was after my money and stopped as soon as I threw cash at him. I then ran out of the room."

"I think you did the right thing, Raja."

"I do want to go back and teach him a lesson, though. Each scar on my body reminds me of him," Raja said wrathfully.

"I would like to see them."

"What?"

"Your scars."

The air inside the room filled with an awkward silence.

"Do you think they might be looking for you?"

"Who?"

"Your parents."

Raja looked up into the man's eyes with a sarcastic smile. "No one gives a shit about no one around here *sahib*! My stepfather doesn't even care if I live or die. He must be missing all the money he won't be getting from me, but no more. My mother, she is too busy pleasing her new husband. She is probably done crying over me by now," Raja said in a cold, incensed voice. "The street is my home now; this is where I belong."

"Would you believe me if I told you that I care about you, Raja?" man asked. "You can share anything you want with me."

It started to rain outside. Strong wind carried the drops and slammed them against the walls. The sound of falling rain surrounded the room, mixed in with cricket noise. Raja wished his brother would come back soon. His mind drifted back to the morning at the market square. Raja and his brother had hurried to pick the busiest spot where the majority of the foot traffic was.

"Will you hurry up, lazy bones?" Raja's brother, Saif, scolded him. Raja scurried behind his brother. Saif, three years older than Raja, was tall and scrawny. His long, thick, curly hair went all the way down to the base of his neck. He walked with a limp caused by the polio he had contracted as a child. Saif had left home a couple of years before Raja. Before he'd left, he would put a hand on Raja's mouth and drag him under the covers whenever they saw their stepfather chasing their screaming, teary-eyed mother around the house in the middle of the night. He'd understood when Raja showed up one day at a work site and said, "I am not going back home."

Both brothers woke up every morning and went to work: windshield cleaning of cars stopped at traffic lights, hauling farmers' produce and meat to market in the city, lugging bricks at a construction site. Raja shadowed his brother for a while before he was declared ready to take a job on his own.

"If we get there before anyone else, we might get picked right away. Early morning jobs are usually easy, and they pay well."

The merciless month of August in the city of Lahore was living up to its reputation. Monsoon season built the heat and humidity during the day before drenching the city with a downpour in the evening. It was sweltering, humid, and not a single breath of air was felt. Drops of sweat fell from the tips of noses and the foreheads of even those who sat motionless. It was almost eight in the morning by the time the brothers got to the market square, a large gathering place encircling a tall minaret, which was a historical landmark, built in commemoration of the Pakistan revolution. It was a blend of Mughal and modern architecture. The site was encircled by acres of grass and plantation. Aside from being a busy tourist attraction, the area was well known for day laborers and kite flyers. It was swamped with street urchins looking for work. They hustled and bid for the lowest price to the potential customers who walked among them and picked the one perfect for the job. From moving furniture, painting walls, cutting grass, to hauling groceries, there was help available for everything, cheap.

Raja and his brother made their way through the crowd to claim their favorite spot, hurriedly munching on the bread and gulping down the tea they grabbed on the way. Saif cursed under his breath when he saw two other street urchins there.

"Shit, we are late!" He ground his teeth. "That happens when you crawl like a turtle instead of rushing." Saif gave Raja a scornful look.

"Don't start a fight. We can move to a different spot." Raja sensed the temper rising in his brother.

"Not sure where we will go."

"Maybe we can look for it together," Raja suggested.

"No. You go sit by the stairs and wait for me. I will find a spot and come and get you." Saif pointed to the white marble stairs in the distance, leading up to the minaret.

"But I am ready!"

"Like hell you are. We are already late. I don't have the time to find work for both of us."

Raja did not see the point in arguing with his brother and nodded.

Raja unbuttoned the top of his shirt and fanned himself, sitting at the marble stairs that marked the entrance to the minaret. The place had already started to fill in. Raja gazed around and saw a few tourists with cameras hanging from their necks. They were always easy to work with, he was told, and they paid well. Soon his attention was captured by two kites, red and blue, flying in the sky, diving, soaring, and crisscrossing each other. They were in a match. The rivals on the ground used their skills and techniques to cut through each other's glass-edged strings. They sensed the wind direction and swirled their kites to take the lead. Raja, captivated, placed his hand on his forehead to create an awning, right above his eyes, to get a better look at the duel taking place in the sky.

"Eh, *bacha*! You don't seem to be trying too hard, if you are looking for work," a voice said to his right. Raja looked up. He had to squint his eyes to see two teenagers standing in front of the sun.

"Are you looking for work?" the other teen asked. They were both young, barely eighteen.

One of them had a scar running down his left cheek and a mole under his nose. The other seemed taller and had a moustache. Raja saw his brother negotiating work with a customer and sprang up.

"Yes, *sahib*, I am," Raja answered excitedly. The kites above him soared once again, pulled by the wind, viciously engaged in battle.

"Then how come you are not hustling like everyone else?" The man with the scar on his face sounded doubtful.

"I was just taking a quick break. I am ready for work, *sahib*, I am," Raja replied.

The kites' shadows ran across Raja as they glided into the sky. He wanted to look up and see the direction they were going. He imagined them tangled into each other, rolling, sliding, trying to cut each other loose.

"My boss there needs help. You will need to go to his house." Raja gazed past the two men and saw another man standing at a distance, wearing dark glasses and nicely pressed clothes. He seemed older than his assistants. Raja nodded in agreement.

Kites fluttered right above him. He could hear the thin, tense paper against the wind. Straight ahead on the ground, two rival teenagers tightened the strings, jerking their kites to the side, maneuvering to position them to have an advantage over each other. It will soon be over, Raja thought.

And then a crowd roared "*Bo Kata* — a declaration of victory. Raja saw the defeated red kite, lifeless without the string, floating away into the sky. A few children sprinted in that direction to catch the kite.

"I am the right person for the job, *sahib*. I work hard and will complete the job to your liking." Raja made the sales pitch. The idea of landing the job on his own excited him. He was told that the man needed some boxes to be moved and to clean the place a little.

"Nervous?" Saif asked as he learned that Raja had found work.

"A little bit."

"Don't be. It will be over before you know it."

"Wish you were coming with me," Raja said, as he turned to go with his employers.

"Take this." Saif unhooked the bracelet from his arm and put it on his brother's wrist. "This will mean I am with you all the time. I will go with you to the house to see it, and then come pick you up as soon as I finish work, okay?" Raja agreed. Saif gently ruffled Raja's hair. "Don't be nervous. It will be over soon."

Saif's words echoed in his ears as he sat on the *charpoy*. I wish *bhai* would hurry along, Raja thought.

"Your brother is probably waiting for the storm to be over. It is nasty out there," the man said in a calm voice, as if he read Raja's thoughts. That startled Raja. "It is the beginning of monsoon season, you know."

"What is the job I am here to do?" Raja asked. He felt the rush to get out of there.

"Soon, Raja! Soon you will find out what you are here to do for me," the man replied. "I appreciate your patience."

"I will need some money in advance before I can stay any longer."

The man reached into his pocket and took out some cash. "Will this be enough for now?" He waved a few bills in front of Raja.

The sight of crisp bills brought a shimmer to Raja's eyes. He cautiously got up from the bed and walked up to the man.

"Yes, I think so." Raja grabbed the money from the man's hand and quickly stuffed it in his pants pockets. Money in the pocket made Raja feel a little secure, his first earned wage in a long time. He slowly turned to go back to his seat. In a mechanical motion, his eyes roamed at the right wall in front of him and froze. He squinted his eyes to soak in as much light as he could to make sense of what he was seeing. The dim light inside the room was not enough to get a better view.

"What ... *sahib* ... is this?" Raja mumbled under his breath and edged forward, his gaze fixated on the wall in front of him.

There were pictures, so many of them, pasted across the wall, covering it almost entirely. Raja inched toward the wall to get a closer look. The subjects were all boys, close to his age. Some seemed younger than him. There were faces scattered all over the wall. Some of them were smiling nervously. Others had long, tense facial expressions. Raja wondered who they were. He took a step back and bumped into the man, who was now standing right behind him. A chill ran down Raja's spine.

"Who are they?" he asked, hoping the man did not notice the tremble in his voice. A display of fear was a sign of weakness, he learned on the street.

"Have you seen anything like this before, Raja?" the man asked.

"Can't say that I have."

"Can you believe all these pictures are of my friends?"

"They are your friends?"

"All my friends," man replied, "just like you."

"I am not your friend. I am here to do a job for you."

"Don't be stubborn, Raja. I can tell from your troubled past that you don't have many friends. I would very much like to be your friend," the man said and placed his hands on Raja's shoulders.

"Sooner I start the job, sooner I will be able to leave—"

"Aren't you going to ask me my name?"

"Why?"

"I asked for yours. You think it is fair?"

"What is your name?"

"I am glad you asked, dear boy." The man's hands firmed onto Raja's shoulders.

"Where are your friends now?" Raja ignored the man's comments, his chest suddenly pounding with rapid heartbeats.

"They are all gone to places they were destined to."

"Do you see them again?"

"They do not come back once they leave, just like you, Raja. Once you leave here, you will not come back," the man replied. "Isn't it sad?"

"I ... don't—"

"I treated them so well. But when they left, they never looked back. I do suspect that will be the case with you. That is why I would like to remember you by taking a picture of you before you leave." The man's voice lowered to a mere whisper.

"Are you going to display my picture on the wall as well, just like the rest of them?"

"It is my way of remembering my friends, yes," the man replied.

Among all the pictures on the wall, two captured Raja's attention the most, and his facial expression tightened. The boys in the photos looked familiar. First was Daud, the boy he had met last year. Daud went missing last month. The second photograph was of Rehman, the very first boy Raja had met when he landed on the streets, aside from his brother. Rehman was a couple of years older than he, had short-cropped hair and dense black eyes. Raja had sat on Rehman's bicycle-frame bar, grabbing the handle tightly, while Rehman rode the bike around town. They stopped and got *bhutta* (corn on the cob) before resting by the Lahore canal. At night, Rehman took Raja to his home, one of the many large sewer pipes lined up on the west end of the city underneath the Ravi River bridge. New developments and modernization had led the city to adopt a more advanced sewer system and shift the flow of the waste to south side of town, leaving giant concrete sewer pipes abandoned and dry. It soon became the perfect refuge for street urchins and the homeless. They all paid rent to the local mob to live in those pipes. Raja and Rehman played *Ludo* — a dice-rolling board game — and talked about girls.

"Ever touched a woman's breasts?" Rehman asked Raja.

"No." Raja made a face.

"Ever want to?"

"Um ... Maybe."

"Tomorrow we'll go to Anarkali Bazaar." Rehman lit a cigarette. "It is packed midday with women. All you do is pretend that you slipped, and then run your hands on as many breasts as you like." He winked and passed the cigarette on to Raja.

No one had seen Rehman for days. Raja went back several times to see if Rehman was back at his pipe. He ran into the rent collector one of those times, who was looking for Rehman also.

"Tell that little rat to show up and pay the money," he bellowed at Raja. "Or I will see to it that he ends up serving tea and passing out condoms at the brothels for the rest of his life."

Rehman was smiling in the picture. What happened to him, Raja wondered. He wanted to ask the man about him, but the words got stuck in his throat. Something was not right.

"I ... I need more water!" Raja could barely utter the words. The man handed him back the glass. It was warm now. It made him feel sick in his stomach.

"Are you ready for your photo, Raja?" The man's grip got firmer on his shoulder.

"I ... am not feeling well ... I—"

"Let me help you." The man took Raja back to the bed. "Sit here, smile, and I will take your picture."

"I am too weak to do any work for you. Maybe I can come back tomorrow." Raja said in a weak voice. His head was spinning.

"Tomorrow is too far away, my friend," the man responded. "Besides, you have the money in your pocket. Stay a little longer, Raja." The room suddenly felt darker than before to Raja. "We are so close, so close to the end. How can we possibly let this moment pass? Soon you will be free. We will all be free, trust me. Just let me take this picture." The man dug into his pants pocket and took out a camera. It was small 35-millimeter disposable camera with a built-in flash. "Look at the camera, Raja! Look and smile. I bet no one ever took your picture before." The man grinned as he pressed the camera against his eyes.

"I recognize one of the photos on the wall." The words seemed to roll off Raja's tongue though he did not intend to say them.

The man's finger stopped at the shutter of the camera.

"Who?"

"Rehman. His picture is on the wall on the lower right corner. Where is he?" Raja wondered if he had made a mistake by mentioning Rehman to the man. But it was too late.

"You know him?"

"Yes."

"Ah, Rehman! Of course... . Yes, he was here, just like you. Now he is gone."

"He did not come back," said Raja.

"He could be closer to you than you know, *bacha*."

"I don't know what that means." Raja shrugged his shoulders.

"I can never tell where someone will go once they leave here. Do you expect me to know that?" A moment of silence passed. "He was peaceful when he left here. I am sure he is happy now wherever he is," the man replied. "How exciting! It is time to take your picture."

Before Raja could say anything further, the flash went off and the entire room was flooded with bright white light for less than a second. Raja squinted his eyes as too much light entered his retinas. He rubbed his eyes as if to release excess light from them. His fingers stopped at the sight of the man, who was now standing right next to him, staring straight into his eyes. The man sat down on the *charpoy* next to him.

"You are a brave little boy," the man said, "so young, yet strong, resolute, almost to the point of being arrogant. You fear, but you don't show it. You feel pain, but you don't wince. You get hurt, but you take it in stride, as what life has thrown at you."

"I ... I don't know what—" Raja mumbled.

"It is all around us, just like the rain outside, pain, suffering, misery, drenching us all in it. It envelops us and never leaves. You are so young, fresh, full of life. And yet, you are caught in the vicious circle of this cruel life," the man said. "I am like you, my little friend, a victim of this society."

Raja's eyes grew heavier. He wondered if it was the heat and tropical humidity making him drowsy. Then he thought of his empty stomach and realized he hadn't had anything to eat since this morning. Finally, he looked at the glass and wondered what was in it that he'd been drinking. He remembered feeling this way once when he sniffed glue. He desperately wiped sweat from his face.

"I didn't tell you."

"Tell me what?"

"My name," the man replied. "You asked me my name. My, name, ... is Javed Iqbal." His face was now inches away from Raja.

Raja's head swayed in slow motion. He had lost awareness of his surroundings. A strong smell of the man's body odor entered his nostrils. Sounds of falling rain echoed in his ears like a drum playing at a distance. He looked into the man's eyes, becoming aware of why he was brought here.

"You *harami*!"

"Shhh, *bacha*!" the man placed a finger on his lips, "it is easy if you don't struggle." Raja flinched and tried to push away.

"I bet your picture will look great on that wall." The man chuckled and clapped his hands.

Raja tried to get up. The man's hand slammed against Raja's cheek and slapped him back to *charpoy*. A pool of blood gathered under his skin. Raja quivered. His eyes widened as he saw the man closing in on him, pushing him down with his weight. In a flash of a second, Raja was pinned to the *charpoy*, Javed leaning on top of him.

"Let me go!" Raja tried to shout. But his famished body could only afford a meager screech.

Echoes of Javed's panting and Raja's scream bounced back from the walls of the nearly empty room.

"What happened to brave Raja?" Javed snickered.

The man rolled Raja over to his stomach.

The woven ropes of the *charpoy* pressed against Raja's left cheek, cutting deep, leaving marks on his skin. His mind drifted in and out, wondering what was happening to him.

"Are you afraid, Raja, are you scared?" The man's lips touched Raja's ear as he uttered the words, whispering.

"Please forgive me, *sahib*," Raja begged.

"I think I will like it if you were."

"Take the money back, but let me go." Tears rolled down the sides of his face.

"I begged once, Raja. Just like you." Javed locked Raja's hands behind his back and weighed down with his knee on Raja's struggling legs. "There were two of them; maybe you know them, maybe you don't. But they came from the streets. I treated them with nothing but respect. As a result, they beat me till they thought I was dead, and left me to bleed, alone. And they left, Raja, got lost in the crowd, not to be found again, no matter how hard I searched for them. But I was wrong in trying to look for those two. Do you understand, my friend?" Javed paused to wipe dripping sweat from his face. "They were all around me, and I could not see it. I see them in every photo on the wall." He pointed at the collage. "I see them in you. Because you would do the same thing if I let you, wouldn't you, Raja?"

Raja mumbled something, but words did not come out. His body felt crushed under the weight of the man, and his skin stretched deep into the ropes.

"*Bhai!*" Face down, Raja bellowed and called for Saif.

Outside, a tin roof blew off and slammed against the transom. The storm had intensified.

Javed leaned over and whispered to Raja, "Your brother is not coming."

Raja's muscles tore as if a dagger slowly pierced him. A sharp pain entered his lower abdomen like a fire rushing through his body, moving upwards and exiting through his throat in the form of a scream. Raja tried to spin but was slammed back facedown because of the weight on top of him. His eyes wide, jaws stretched, another stream of tears rolled from his eyes as he tried to fight the pain. His fingers dug through the gap holes of the *charpoy*. His body shivered for a second and then flattened as his muscles stretched. He let out another scream as agonizing pain registered in his brain. He powerlessly tried to set himself free. "Please don't hurt me!" Raja pleaded.

The pain returned, this time more intense. The sound of thunder along with Raja's screams roared all across the room.

"Yes! Scream for life, beg for mercy, please." The man's eyes were bright and wide with a savage look on the face as he grunted. He tightened his grip around Raja as Raja slammed his head against the *charpoy* in pain.

"Why beg for this life, Raja, which betrayed you? It let you down. Pain is the road to salvation," the man exclaimed.

Everything seemed blurry. Raja tried to scream once more, but this time it was more like a groan, vibrating sound waves constantly shaking his body. His throat felt slashed. The face of his brother came before his eyes. He wondered if Saif was looking for him, if anyone out there was looking for him. More tears rolled from his eyes. But the pain was subdued now. His body was numb. Time had elapsed. There was no counting of seconds, minutes, or hours. Bleakly, Raja heard the sound of the man in the background, laughing and yelling; his body swayed aimlessly on the *charpoy*.

This is temporary, he assured himself; it will soon be over. His mind tried to placate the pain with pleasant thoughts. A red kite flew in his mind, in a cloudless blue sky: dodging, soaring high, and counting on the skill of the string holder down below. Its thin paper fluttered against the wind, trying to stay afloat. But with just one sharp cut, detached from the string that held it, beyond the control of the kite flyer, it swayed aimlessly, gliding away, descending, only to be snatched, maybe torn, by several hands chasing it on the ground.

Outside, water dripped from soaked tree leaves into overflowing ponds and flooded streets. The rain had stopped; the rushing wind had subsided. Raja stopped weeping; he was done pleading.

The door slammed open, and two teenagers walked in. The grim light of fast-approaching dusk crawled into the room. With delusional mind and numb body, Raja tried to half-open his eyes, hoping to see his brother. Through blurry vision, all he could see was two shadows approaching the bed.

"What in God's name did you do to him?" one of them said, looking at Raja.

Both teens must have been out in the rain; their clothes were damp. Raja's brain, through the haze of pain and intoxication, recalled them from early that morning. They were the ones who had come up to him and offered work. They stood by the bed as Javed tried to regain his breath.

"So nice of you to come back, my little angels" Javed looked at his accomplices and smiled.

Raja's body recoiled. Pain had returned. He wanted to move, but every inch of his body felt swollen. He could see all three of them standing around him. Their voices echoed in his ears, but he could not understand the words. His heart was pounding heavily. His head spun as his mind slowly realized what had happened to him. Raja tried to speak, but no sound came out. His throat felt like it was scratched against bed of thorns.

"Water!" he said in barely audible voice.

Javed glanced at him and leaned over. He ran his hand across Raja's face. "Yes, indeed! Someone get this *bacha* some water."

Raja lay there motionless, without any emotion on his face; he gazed at Javed's face as it leaned over him. Raja's eyes did not blink. Javed grabbed the bottle of water handed to him by one of his accomplices. Dried crust chipped away as Raja's lips parted. Javed slowly poured drops of water in Raja's mouth. Raja's body felt irrigated.

His muscles relaxed. Raja sprinkled a few drops on Raja's face.

"Relax, *bacha*. Looks like the storm is over, almost." Javed ran his fingers through Raja's hair. He then looked at two newcomers. "Make sure he does not leave"

Both accomplices closed in on Raja. Dark shadows of fear swelled into Raja's eyes.

Javed calmly walked out of the room to a veranda, surrounded by white, calcium-covered, red brick walls. Right in the middle was a leafless tree, its trunk rooted way deep into the muddy ground around it. He walked up to the spigot attached to an external water pipe and ran his hands under the cold running water. The air was filled with the smell of wet mud and fresh grass. There were voices coming from the room, some loud, some subdued. Javed fished in the pants pocket with the camera in it and took out a pack of cigarettes. He lit a cigarette and walked away, leaving behind gray smoke dancing in the air.

. . .

Her heart skipped a beat when she opened her eyes and stared at the ceiling. What caused her to wake up so abruptly, she wondered. Must have been a bad dream, she thought. The storm had passed. All was quiet around her except for the faint barking of a dog in the distance and her husband snoring inside the room. She flicked the light switch up and down a couple of times and gave up. There was no electricity in the house. Lightning must have knocked down the main power line. Still in bed, she ran her hand in the dark and searched for candles to light. Pots and pans transformed into dark shadows bopping on the walls through flickering flames of yellow candlelight. She slowly got up and walked up to the window. Her heart was beating too fast. She looked outside and gazed at the dark night. The sky had cleared, and stars were visible. Leaves on the tree rustled in a calm rhythm with the wind. The road outside was still wet and burnished. Something wasn't right. Something had gone wrong in the dark shadows of the black night. But she did not know what it was. She said a silent prayer for her sons, out there, living in the street. She had not seen the younger of her two sons for almost a month now. She had cried in the beginning. Eventually her tears dried, and she cried only in her heart, missing, longing for her offspring, her Raja. She remembered the night he had woken her up. It was the middle of the night.

"*Amma*! Wake up!" She felt someone shaking her shoulder. There was a black bruise right underneath Raja's left eye, and his forehead was swollen.

"What's wrong?" She rubbed her eyes, half asleep. Then she saw the bruises. "Did he hit you again?" She fingered through his hair to take a better look at the injury.

"Are you awake?"

"How can I sleep now?"

"It's nothing new."

"Oh, *beta*, I wish I could change things." Her voice started to choke.

"This was the last time," Raja said with a cold, stony face.

"Come, lie down with me," she offered.

Raja placed his hands on hers and pressed firmly.

"I am so sorry, son. I wish I could …"

"Don't say anything. It's not your fault."

"Let me put some ice on it."

"I don't have time, *amma*! I am leaving," Raja said.

She sat up in bed and dashed her palm against her forehead.

"Don't leave," she wept.

"If I stay, I will murder him."

"Shut your mouth!" she cried.

"I have seen how he beats you."

Her lips trembled in anguish, but no words came out.

"I don't know where I am going. But I have to leave now."

"Can't you wait till the dawn?" she pleaded with her son.

"*Amma*, I am not leaving to come back," Raja replied. He sounded resolute. The words landed like a hammer on her head.

"What?! What do you …" She could not finish the sentence.

"I am going to live with *bhai*."

She sat in bed and rocked in grief from left to right.

"I am not coming back, *amma*. Do you understand?

Tears rolled down her face. Her mouth was open, eyes begging her son not to go. She had cooked him a meal before watching him walk out the squeaky hinged door.

It had been weeks now since she last saw him. She took comfort in knowing that his older brother was with him and would bring her news of his wellbeing. But tonight was different than previous nights. Something inside her told her Raja was not fine. She cupped her hands and offered another prayer, and went back to bed.

. . .

The sounds of crickets and cicadas were deafening. The warm, muggy night was inviting for critters all around. A rickshaw drove past the corner as Javed walked back into the house. It was dark. There were light posts on the street, but were not working. He peeked through the crack in the door before closing it behind him. He walked past the veranda toward the room. It was quiet. There was no sound of any movement inside. He slowly opened the door.

Raja was lying on the floor, half unconscious, curled up in a fetal position. There was a small pool of blood next to him. The two teens were sitting on the bed, smoking. They all exchanged glances, but no one said anything. Javed walked up to Raja and hunkered down next to him. He stared at his pale face. Raja lay motionless. Javed dipped his fingers in the blood.

"He tried to escape," one of the accomplices said sheepishly. Javed pressed his other finger against Raja's neck to feel his pulse. Outside, a dog started barking.

"He is as good as dead. Look at him!" the older of the two accomplices said, exhaling the smoke. "A few more hours like this and he'll be gone."

"Get busy, both of you," Javed said to him.

Both accomplices proceeded to the two large metal containers in the room and dug out a metal chain from between them. With calculated steps, one of them walked over to Javed and handed him the chain.

Javed grabbed the chain and slowly coiled it around Raja's neck. Now there were two dogs, barking uncontrollably.

"Can you two freeloaders go out and take care of those fucking dogs?!" Javed bellowed.

Both teenagers scurried out.

"Stab them if you have to. Make them stop," Javed shouted over his shoulder.

"My apologies, little Raja, for taking this long to show you why you are here"

Javed rolled both ends of the chain around his hands and tightened his grip.

"Will it matter to you if I told you, you are the most special of all my friends? I am afraid there will be no other after you. But I will always remember you." Raja breathed heavily as the metal chain snaked around his neck slowly.

Javed leaned over to Raja and spoke, "I will tell your brother how sweet you were, if I see him." Raja's hand fluttered as Javed tightened the chain around his neck. Raja's body half raised with the tension around his neck. Raja's face turned red, and his eyes widened, staring at the wall in front of him. The faces on the photos posted on the wall were looking back at him. His fingers desperately tried to pry the chain open. There were no questions left in his eyes. His face was robbed of any emotions as he looked at Javed. His fingers slipped away from the chain. Soon Raja stopped moving. The man continued to squeeze the chain around

Raja's neck for few more seconds, panting, before letting it loose. Raja's body plummeted back on to the floor.

Minutes later, cold water ran out of the tap in the veranda, changing color as it drained while Javed rinsed off blood from his hands. The door opened, and the two accomplices walked out of the room into the veranda. They hastily walked up to the tap and joined their leader.

"Are we clear?"

"Yes, we are," one of them replied, just like every other time."

"This time, you leave," Javed said with his back toward them. "And do not come back."

They both looked at each other.

"Get rid of these clothes and leave town, tonight," Javed said.

"But, we thought we could—" the other teen tried to protest, but was interrupted by Javed.

"Don't you see? It is over - the storm is over. It is all clear now, my dear." Javed gently slapped their cheeks.

"Have your last meal in the city, take the bus and travel north."

"You are making us nervous."

"Do as I say and you will be safe." Javed closed the spigot and shook dripping water off his fingers. "Wherever you go, do not mention this house — or me — to anyone."

. . .

The room was lit with the same faded light coming from the bulb hanging down from the ceiling. It was awfully quiet. Javed finished writing the letter and tilted his face to the ceiling, his eyes closed, his demeanor calm. His fingers tapped the chair arm, one at a time, in a rhythmic motion. He was alone in the room. His accomplices had left per his instructions. The chaos and screams that enveloped the room earlier played in his ear. He finally opened his eyes and took out a picture from his pants pocket. It was Raja's photo; he was serious and somewhat apprehensive, staring at the camera. Javed ran his fingers across the picture and stared at it for a while before getting up and walking over to the wall to his right. He stood in front of the wall covered with pictures of young boys. All he had to do now was to find one last spot on the already-filled wall, one more corner to fill in with Raja's photo. He turned the picture over and wrote, "100. "

3 LAHORE

February 7, 1998

It was late afternoon when bus arrived at the station. Daud was sound asleep. His head rested on Yosef's shoulder. The shrieking sound of brakes woke him up as the bus came to a halt. They waited for other passengers to get off before exiting. It was overcast and cold, but wasn't snowing. Dark shades of gray had blanketed the city.

"We have arrived," Yosef spoke.

In front of their eyes was a vast urban sprawl, crawling with millions of living beings on foot, in cars, on motorcycles and rickshaws, and in horse-drawn carts. Intimidated, overwhelmed, nervous—they felt all of that as they looked around and stood there for a while. It was not the town of twelve hundred residents they left behind. Daud clenched his hand on Yosef's arm and stared in awe. Alleys and cobblestone streets stretched in all directions with no pattern or grid. Nearby, a bazaar was set up, with shops full of colorful fabrics and toys, and shimmering lights hanging from the storefront walls. Small shops and hawkers hollered and solicited passersby to buy their food or goods. Some of the local hawkers had stretched their shops and stands out to the street. Two tall bamboo shoots were erected on each side of each store. Tied to the upper edge of the shoots was tarpaulin-type fabric stretched on top to create an awning. It was a concrete jungle with houses and apartments sprawling through each and every single inch of land available.

Right outside the bus stop was a hole-in-the-wall *dhaba* (a roadside diner), unpretentious, made of mud, furnished with tables and wooden benches. The smell of grilled chicken and fresh *naan* (flatbread) coming out of the clay oven wafted into their nostrils. Daud tugged Yosef's shirt.

"Let's eat." Yosef looked at him and smiled.

The diner was warm inside. Wooden benches and tables were occupied by the customers being served. There was an open kitchen at the far end of the diner, and a large man with a thick mustache sat at the register. A female singer's voice came through the loudspeakers. They could not make out the dialect she was singing in, amid the loud buzzing sound of people eating and chatting around them. The diner was packed, and there was only one waiter serving all the customers. Yosef sighted two spots at the outer edge of one of the benches by the window. They took the seats and waited to order food.

"Are you okay?" Yosef looked at Daud, whose head was down.

"I don't know," he replied.

"Hungry?"

"Maybe."

"Anything else?"

"I feel alone," Daud said.

"Miss your family?"

Daud nodded.

"But you were without them in the factory, also."

A cold draft entered through the poorly sealed window. Daud put his hands on his biceps, covering his chest.

"We should get warmer clothes."

"I know just the place," the waiter said as he approached them. "May I also suggest *keema* (ground beef) with green peas and *naan*? They are just delicious."

He was scrawny, short, and agile, with a pointy nose, long black uncombed hair, about their age. He wiped his hands on the tattered rag hanging from the back pocket of his black trousers, and took out a small notepad and pencil, ready to take their order.

"So what is it going to be?"

"You said something about getting warm clothes?"

"First time to Lahore?" the waiter asked.

"We can use a recommendation."

"Landa Bazaar," the waiter responded. "Just to the west, past the railway station."

"Thank you."

"Need a place to stay?"

"I think we will be okay."

"Hummm!" The waiter glanced at the bag sitting on Daud's lap. "Hungry?"

They ate chicken grilled in herbs and spices; whipped plain yogurt mixed with chunks of cucumber, tomatoes, and onion; and flatbread brought to them fresh from the oven. The steam rising from the food momentarily made them forget the long, tiring, bone-aching trip they had taken on the bus to Lahore. Hunger took over and they ate in silence, energizing their famished bodies.

"Did … you kill him?" Daud eventually asked. His question caught Yosef as he was wiping his mouth with a wet rag. Yosef stared at him. "And the money in the bag. Is it his?"

"How about a 'Thank you for digging me out of that shithole'?" he snapped.

"I did not mean to upset you," Daud replied. "You shoved me out of the room. I want to know what you did to Akbar."

"If you are that concerned, the same bus that brought us here will be leaving shortly to go back to Mingora." Yosef leaned forward. "Want me to buy you a one-way ticket back?

"No … please."

"Then what?"

"I will be quiet from now on."

They sat in silence for a while. Yosef stared at Daud as customers ate and left the restaurant and others came in.

"Are you afraid?" Yosef eventually asked.

"What?"

"Are you afraid that he might come after us?"

"I am afraid, yes, but not of him."

"What are you afraid of?"

"Of being alone."

"I guess being with me is not much of a comfort."

"This is all new to me."

"For me, too."

"And yes, I fear he might come for us."

"We are far away. He can't reach us."

"So, you …?"

"Let's just say Akbar will live, but wish he didn't." With his fingernail, Yosef tried to remove a piece of chicken stuck between his teeth, and offered a grin.

The waiter returned to pick up the empty plates.

"Anything else?" he asked.

"Just the bill." Yosef motioned Daud to take some money out from the bag. The waiter took the chair right next to them and sat down.

"I work at this restaurant six days a week," he said. "I watch buses arrive at the depot by the hour. And I witness the passengers who get off, change busses, or get on."

"What's your point?"

"Point is, my friend, that I have seen your type getting on and off these buses many times. Don't think it isn't obvious."

"What isn't?"

"That you are a runaway, running from something or someone."

"Wow. You have such great talent at being a psychic. Yet you are still nothing but a raggedy waiter," Yosef snickered.

"You think, now you are here, you know everything?"

"I suppose if I ask you, you will tell me everything there is to know, right?"

"You need protection."

"Shouldn't you be waiting on other customers right now?" Yosef laughed.

"If you think you will be able to walk past Landa Bazaar with whatever you are carrying in the bag" — the waiter pointed at the bag — "you are mistaken."

"Thanks for the tip."

"Meet me after my shift, and I will make sure you don't get lost."

"And if I see you hovering around looking for us later, I will make sure you are left with half your number of teeth by tomorrow." Yosef waved his fist in the air.

"Suit yourself, *sala harami*." Yosef heard the waiter whisper a curse as he walked out the restaurant with Daud.

"Oh my God!" Daud yelped as they walked along the sidewalk. Dusk was upon them. A chill in the air intensified as weak sun rays succumbed to rising shadows.

"What now?"

"What did the waiter want?"

"He wanted to see if the fear and nervousness in your eyes was real."

"I don't know how not to be that obvious," Daud sniffed.

"Just stay close to me, and we will be fine." Yosef put his arms around Daud's shoulders. "One more thing," he said. "I think it is best if I carry the bag from here on."

Yosef and Daud strolled through the side roads and alleys to reach the streets of Old Lahore, also known as the "walled city." It was an ancient sight which, according to some historians, dated as far back as 2000 BCE. The original walls had stood during the time of Mughal Empire and were destroyed by the British in 1849 when they annexed the city. Though eroded by modern development, access to the walled city was still only gained through one of the thirteen ancient gates. Long-winded and quaint streets inside the gates took the boys through areas of old houses with brick facades, flat roofs, richly carved wooden balconies, and overhanging windows. Through one of those thirteen ancient gates, they passed Data Darbar, the mausoleum of a Sufi saint, and went on to Landa Bazaar, the market famous for cheap and used articles.

They strolled alongside a park, fenced and gated with black iron, in front of the railway station. They gazed at an old two-story building covered with hand-painted cinema billboard signs. Daud slid down and sat on the ledge of the iron fence above the sidewalk. Yosef walked over to the street hawker at the corner selling *paan* (betel leaves filled with areca nuts, slaked lime paste, and powdered tobacco) and cigarettes. He ordered two *paans* and four loose cigarettes.

"How do you like your new home, *bacha*?" Yosef asked as he offered the *paan* to Daud. They started walking again.

"This is ours, all of it?"

"Yep, pick a street, a corner, a park where you would like to sleep, and it is yours." Yosef ruffled Daud's glistening black hair.

"What is this?" Daud asked, as he held out the *paan* in his hand.

"Chew it, slowly." Yosef showed how by putting it in his mouth and moving his lower jaw in a circular motion. Daud imitated.

"Now remember, there is a technique to eating *paan*," Yosef taught Daud. "You chew and spit only from the bottom corner of your mouth. Watch."

Yosef chewed the *paan* a few more times. And then, like a pro, he made a slight opening at the bottom left corner of his tightly closed mouth. A brown liquid sprayed out the small opening and splattered on a sidewall.

"Now you try it," he said.

Daud mostly remembered how skillfully Yosef had spat out in a straight line. Impressed, he ignored the burning sensation on his gums from the tobacco and lime paste. A few more rounds of chewing and he was ready to prove he was a quick learner. His jaw moved clockwise one last time, his lips tightened, a small opening appeared at the corner of his mouth, and brown liquid came out. But instead of a power spray, it squirted and drooled down Daud's chin, down his neck right onto his shirt. He squealed. Yosef burst into laughter.

"Whoa! Look at you; you look like a clown monkey!" Yosef exclaimed, laughing and dancing.

Daud wiped the drool with the back of his hand. "I am not a clown monkey."

"You sure can gather a crowd and make some money that way," Yosef teased. Daud wiped his hands on a wall and hurriedly followed Yosef.

They had passed the main road and now were walking along an abandoned railroad tracks. There were scattered settlements of squatters on both sides of the tracks.

"Stay close to me and you will learn all sorts of tricks," Yosef lit two cigarettes and offered one to Daud.

"What is this for?"

"It is to celebrate the beginning of our fucking freedom." Yosef showed Daud how to take a puff. Daud's eyes turned red as he inhaled the smoke and let out a throat-slashing cough. He bent and coughed some more.

"C'mon! You are embarrassing me." Yosef took another puff from his cigarette and laughed at the hunched-over Daud, coughing as if ready to spill his kidneys out. Water ran from Daud's eyes as he tried to calm his breathing down. He could hear how Yosef was amused at the outcome, laughing, giggling, relaxed and exhaling smoke. Daud pressed his stomach trying to slow the coughing, patches of blue smoke still exhaling from his mouth and nostrils. Then he noticed that Yosef had stopped laughing. Daud looked up and saw Yosef's stone-cold face. He was staring into the distance, into the dark.

"What is it?" Daud asked.

"Be quiet." Yosef placed his index finger on his lips.

Daud looked in the direction Yosef was staring and saw four shadows approaching them. A cold tingling sensation ran down his spine.

"Who are they?"

"Stay behind me."

"Who are they?" Daud asked in a terrified voice, looking at four tall boys heading straight for them.

Two chickens darted out of one of the adjacent huts, clucking, pecking in the air, flapping around, running, turning in every direction. Three small children came running out, screaming, their arms spread, chasing the chickens. One of the children dove to catch one and landed right in the dirt. The chicken jumped in the air, flapping its wings right in front of Daud's face. And through dust and flying feathers, Daud saw one of the four boys punching Yosef in the stomach.

They were led into a different neighborhood, quiet and dark, a sharp contrast to where they had been few hours ago. The majority of the windows on the adjacent buildings were either boarded or secured with vertical iron bars. Some of the apartments had front balconies and terraces with cracked plaster. On the ends of the balconies, washed clothes hung on tight ropes, swinging in the breeze. The door of a grocery store on the left side of the street was completely covered with graffiti and political slogans. Four men sat outside the store on a cement bench, playing cards and drinking tea. They seemed unconcerned with Daud and Yosef being dragged away and continued to drink their tea. There was an unpaved portion in the middle of the street where muddy rainwater had accumulated. Each time a taxi or rickshaw drove into that pot hole, water splashed to the side, making the sideways and any unfortunate passerby wet.

They came upon a *gali* (alley), dark and narrow, and Yosef and Daud were shoved into it by the hands clawed at the backs of their necks. They walked between the dingy and slimy walls, which were barely an inch away from their shoulders. The air around the alley was filled with the stench of urine and feces. The *gali* widened, and there were several garbage dumpsters placed against the grimy brick walls. Yosef and Daud noticed heads, clusters of them, huddled behind the dumpsters. They belonged to young boys, squatted and crouched on the floor of the *gali*, their heads covered with white cloths. They formed a semicircle and had their backs toward the newcomers. Randomly, one of them would let out a bleak sound, while his body jerked frantically. He then would shake his head for several seconds before returning to a calm state.

It created a strange rhythm of motion as their bodies moved sporadically, inhaling from yellow paper bags, while the rats scurried on top of the dumpsters. Captivated by their strange behavior, Yosef failed to realize that he had gotten too close to them. During a head-shaking, one of them spotted Yosef, who was now standing only few feet from the group. The boy's bloodshot eyes widened, and he let out a scream as he spotted Yosef staring at them. This sudden noise startled Yosef. He took a step back and backed into his captors. By now all heads were uncovered, and all eyes were watching Yosef. Their faces were stone-white and their eyes red, Yosef noticed. There were a total of seven of them, wearing old tattered clothes. They slowly rose to their feet and started to walk toward Yosef. A cold chill ran through Yosef's bones as he retreated. He ran his hand behind his back to feel and grab hold of Daud, but did not find him. Daud was standing a few feet behind, closer to the alley entrance, his hands were shaking.

From the far corner of the shadows appeared the waiter from the restaurant. He was with another boy, shorter and thick-bodied. Yosef's eyes widened. Daud recognized the waiter right away and let out a cry.

"I was beginning to wonder when you would reappear, you fucking rat!" Yosef tried to break himself free from the arms of the boys holding him.

"I never vanished. You just couldn't see me," the waiter responded nonchalantly, gnawing on a piece of sugar cane. He pointed out Yosef to the short boy and stepped back into the darkness.

"My name is Meera," he grabbed Yosef by the chin and introduced himself. "New to town, I hear?"

"Looks like that dog of yours that you have as pet has already filled you in," Yosef snickered.

"Yes, yes, he mentioned you have some tongue on you. So far, he is proving to be right, you know," Meera smiled.

Meera's long, black, wavy, shaggy hair covered half of his forehead. Facial hair had started to grow around the corners of his upper lips. The brown of his skin had gotten darker with layers of dry sweat and humidity. He ran his left fingers along his clearly visible jawbones and chin.

"You walk through my street, you have to pay the dues." Meera circled Yosef.

"Let's decide who shall pay who, yeah?" Yosef fought to set himself free. "What do you say, just you and me, outside, now."

"I admire your courage. But in this town, it means you are stupid," Meera laughed. "I will take what is in the bag on your shoulder. You join my gang. I give you protection."

"How about we decide who is the boss after I break you in two?"

One of the boys holding Yosef jabbed him right below his appendix. Yosef bent and dropped to his knees on the ground.

"Who is that you have with you?" Meera pointed at Daud.

Yosef raised his head and saw a pale and frightened Daud being dragged toward Meera.

"I can take the money from you anytime, and you know it. But I want to have some fun first," Meera leaned over and whispered in Yosef's ears.

"You mother fuc—" Another punch landed directly on Yosef's right ear and lower temple. He grunted in pain and rolled on the ground.

"Come, come here, *bacha*." Meera grabbed Daud by the shoulder. "What is your name?"

Daud's lips trembled, but no words came out.

"A little louder, yes, you are such a nice little boy." Meera's ear touched Daud's lips.

"Daud," he whispered.

"Pretty name for a pretty boy. Is he your older brother?" Meera pointed toward Yosef. Yosef tried to get up, but was pinned down by Meera's shoe crushing his cheekbones.

"Get down on your knees, little Daud." Meera pushed Daud to the ground.

From the corner of his eye, Yosef saw Daud kneeling on the ground. The dim moonlight made the tears on Daud's face looked like melted mercury running down his cheeks.

Three other boys joined Meera and formed a circle around Daud and Meera. Daud's whole body shook when he looked first at Yosef lying on the ground and then into the eyes of the boys encircling him.

"Here is to welcome you, little Daud, to our city and to our gang," Meera spoke. "Hopefully you will be wiser than your brother."

Their hands moved down from their waists, and they unzipped their pants.

"Stay still and it won't get messy," Meera said, hovering right above Daud. "Ever been peed on before?" The other three boys burst into laughter.

Even the rats had sensed the tension in the air and disappeared behind the dumpster. The milky white light of the moon was fading fast against the blue dark The reflection of the street light was projecting toward the front of the left wall.

Yosef wondered what the gang would do to Daud if he said no. He imagined that, in a few minutes, he would be lying on the ground, stabbed in the chest multiple times, drowning in his own blood. He imagined watching, through blurry and weakening vision, the gang chasing after Daud. The thought ran chills through his body as he quivered.

"I would like to see you try that!" A roaring voice came from above and put a halt to the laughter.

Amid the gutters and downspouts was a tall, slender boy dangling from the overhanging wooden porch, slanting toward the alley. He gripped the wooden bar for support and swayed back and forth like a monkey. His physical features were hard to distinguish in the dark, but his athletic agility was obvious.

"Do I need to remind you this is my territory!" Meera growled. "Tell me why I shouldn't shred you into pieces for violating our treaty."

"You touch me, and my gang, waiting right outside this alley, will swarm in, ready to spill your guts out."

The boy dangling from the porch swayed toward the wall, gained momentum by pushing his legs against it, leaped in the air doing a back flip, and landed on the dumpster beneath him. He extended his arms to maintain balance upon landing.

"These two boys are with me. Hand them over."

Appearing close to sixteen years old, he was strong and broad-shouldered, with white skin, green eyes, and dirty blonde hair. He wore faded jeans tattered at the bottom and a red Cossack hat. He knew all too well that stepping into a rival gang's territory could mean instant death. And the members of his gang did not know where he was at that moment. If Meera called his bluff, he most certainly would die, he thought.

"You do not want to harm them," he said in a calm voice, jumping off the dumpster onto the ground.

"Who the fuck are they to you?" Meera bellowed.

"That is not for you to ponder, my little friend."

The comment about Meera's lack of height infuriated Meera.

"I say we cut him right here, boss," one of the boys standing next to Meera growled. Meera turned and slapped him in the face with the back of his hand. The boy almost flew into the wall.

"You come in here," Meera returned his gaze to the tall blonde, "in my territory, insulting me in front of my people, asking me to give up fresh meat?"

"Well ... It is true, what you said."

"What is in it for me?"

Yosef was now resting against the wall. He breathed heavily. Daud ran up to him and held his hand.

"One month. You and your gang can work in my territory. No surcharge, no restriction, you take whatever you make."

"And the police?"

"It will be business as usual for them. I will make sure of that."

Meera chewed on these words for a moment. It wasn't the best, yet not the worst, deal Meera had come across. Given the fact he was face-to-face with one of the most powerful and influential gang leaders in the city, letting go of two street urchins seemed like the best option.

"I'll be seeing your pretty face around." Meera leaned over as he grabbed Yosef's chin and jerked his face.

Reluctantly, the gang retreated. Soon it was only Yosef, Daud, and their rescuer in the alley.

"Grab your bag and let's go."

"Are you Jogi?"

"You are looking at him."

Yosef introduced himself and Daud.

"I know who you are. I was told you would be arriving today. I didn't know you would almost get killed on your first day."

"It was not intentional," Yosef replied.

"Nothing is intentional. Life itself is one big, fucking accident." Jogi smiled and lit a cigarette.

"How did you know how to look for us?" Yosef asked as they walked out the alley. Jogi said he was notified by one of his boys that two new boys had arrived in the city and were later picked by Meera's people.

"I had a hunch that it might be the two boys arriving from Mingora. You are lucky, very lucky, that I got here in time," Jogi said.

They walked alongside each other, away from the alley and onto the street. Jogi occasionally pointed at a few things and told them what they were: an old government building; another vast, iron-fenced park; a famous street. They passed through bazaars where food vendors at grubby food stands sold grilled skewered meet and oven bread. Children crouched on the ground and played *Kanche*, a game of striking small clear marble balls, using the fingers as a sling shot. A little girl brushed the hair of her doll. Nearby, a boy flew paper planes made of scrap notebook paper. A man dashed down some nearby stairs screaming, evidently being chased by his wife holding a skillet, creating a spectacle.

"Is it true what I heard about you?" Jogi asked Yosef.

"What did you hear?"

"That you broke the bones of the carpet factory owner before leaving Mingora."

Yosef dashed a glance toward Daud, who was listening.

"It sounds more dramatic coming from your mouth."

"So it is true."

"You can say that."

"I don't know if I agree with unnecessary violence," Jogi said. "But I can certainly appreciate someone with balls."

Daud walked quietly alongside Yosef and Jogi. His jitters had subsided and he was calm now. The hubbub on the streets had diverted his mind a bit. He had not seen so much commotion on the streets before; things were calm and peaceful in his village. He remembered how he could hear the water current in the Swat River after sunset. He closed his eyes and pictured the snow-capped mountains, green hills, waterfalls. He saw the tall, green, cedar and pine trees sway with the breeze, and the scattered lakes and streams.

And then he bumped into something, or someone. Daud opened his eyes. A boy, close to his age, had snuck up on him from a dark corner and now giggled. Startled, Daud hurled himself closer to Yosef. The boy handed Daud a doll made of bamboo sticks tied together in the middle, shaped like a cross. The ends of the horizontal stick were splintered to make them look like hands. A *pesa* (penny) was glued at the top for the face. It was finished off with a tiny piece of cloth at the very edge: that was a hat. Daud turned to look at the boy, but he swiftly disappeared into the dark. He could hear Yosef and Jogi talking in the background.

"What is your story?" Yosef asked Jogi.

"My story?"

"Yeah, your real story, not the bullshit you throw out on the street."

"You don't think I am legit?"

"A white boy with green eyes and yellow hair, you're definitely not a local."

"Damn! I thought no one would notice."

"Trying dyeing your hair black. That might help you blend in," Yosef laughed.

"You guessed it right. I am not a local."

"Where did you come from?"

"Afghanistan."

"Yeah, you are an Afghani?"

"Why, yes I am. Do you know any?" Jogi asked.

"The camp at the *madrasa* in Madran I went to was run by Afghanis," Yosef reminisced. "Mullah Aziz called them Talibans."

"Taliban," Jogi mumbled under his breath.

"How did you end up here?"

"Different circumstances, but the same way you did." Jogi glanced at Daud, tucked behind Yosef and peeking at Jogi nervously. "What is he to you?"

"He is family."

They approached a *dhaba*. It had ascetic fluorescent lighting, with scattered seating both inside and out. It occupied three storefronts combined, with the middle walls knocked down. A rustic and aged sign hung loosely on the front. The cold wind made it swing; its dried, rusty screws screeched with each sway. The name of the restaurant was Café Pyala (Cup Café). The front of the restaurant was extended out like a veranda. On the far right, a large fire burned inside an elevated clay stove. A big, shallow *tawa* (wok) perched on top of the stove, letting out steam from the liquid simmering in it.

A man sat next to the wok and stirred it occasionally. He was making traditional Kashmiri tea. The air smelled of aromatic seeds of cardamom, cinnamon sticks, and black tea brewing in the milk. The diner was crowded and loud, one corner filled with children of their age. Daud and Yosef followed Jogi, as he seemed to be headed in that direction. Yosef quickly noticed the level of respect Jogi had among those children. Many of them stopped in the midst of their conversation and offered regards. The gesture in their eyes changed as Jogi walked past them.

"You did the right thing," Jogi said in the end, after listening to Yosef's account. He leaned over to Daud and said, "Don't you worry, little boy. No one will lay a hand on you any more."

Daud gave him a sheepish smile. The rest of the time, he sat and looked around the restaurant, trying to listen to the conversations around him, a difficult task to filter through the loud chattering noise that encased the room. Most of the patrons at the restaurant were boys his age or older. They were all scattered around in groups, busy unfolding accounts of their day. Some had food in front of them, others sipped tea only. Some wore old, ragged clothes, had messy hair sticking up, and chewed on their fingernails.

Daud was now one of them. The street was his home. Those boys were like him, runaways. The thought strangely comforted him. He felt he belonged.

"Here is a million-dollar question," Jogi was saying to Yosef. "How are you going to survive on the street?"

"Teach a man how to fish, and you will feed him for rest of his life," Yosef responded. "You show me the way, and I will find work."

By that time, four more urchins had joined the table and conversation.

"You can work alone or join my gang," Jogi said.

"What is the difference?"

"You stay with me, I find you work, I find you where you work, I find you where you live, I show you how to be safe, I teach you how not to get caught by the police." Jogi took a long puff from the cigarette. "You walk on your own, you'll soon learn how to make a living begging, scavenging garbage dumps, picking up half-eaten bones outside the restaurants."

"Or you can find cheaper ways to make money," one of the boys sitting on the table said.

"What is that?"

"You can do *bacha bazi* (sex trade). There are plenty of locals and tourists who will pay lots of money for few minutes worth of—" he could not finish the sentence. Jogi backhand slap to his face sent him to the floor.

"You shut your mouth!"

Jogi then turned to Yosef, "You sell yours or this boy's"—he pointed at Daud—"body for sex, I will personally throw you in front of Meera's gang."

The boy stumbled back up from the floor and ran fingers over his lips to see if there was any blood. "*Sala harami*, who are you to hit me?"

Jogi growled as he flew across the table and jabbed his knee into the boy's chest.

"You're going to tell me how to run my gang?" Jogi's fist, aiming for the boy's face, stopped suspended in the air when he heard another boy calling his name.

"They have got Noora, *dada* (boss)!" a boy at the door exclaimed. "Come quick, they are fighting on the street and are ready for a bloodbath."

"Fuck," Yosef heard Jogi swear under his breath as he rushed out to the street. Yosef motioned Daud to stay put and ran after Jogi.

Out on the street, Noora, a boy from Jogi's gang, was exchanging punches with two other boys from another gang from across town. They had accused Noora of stealing customers from their territory. And they had decided to teach Noora a lesson when he refused to hand over his day's worth of wages. Jogi was quickly filled in with the situation.

Noora's neck was locked between the elbow and forearm of one of the boys, who pummeled Noora in the face. The other boy kicked Noora in the stomach. Noora's arm, dancing through empty air, came upon a red brick sitting on a nearby ledge. He secured the brick in his hand and slammed it against the head of the boy who was punching him in the face. The boy bellowed in pain. A small line of blood snaked down from the back of his head to his neck. The crowd, circled around them, roared at the unexpected turn of events. Noora kneed the boy on the chin, sending him to the ground, then grabbed the other boy by his hair and jumped on his chest.

Jogi tore through the crowd and reached Noora just in time before he slammed the boy's head on to the ground. Jogi grabbed Noora by the collar and dragged him off the boy.

"What the fuck is the matter with you?"

"Let me go, *dada*! I am going to kill those two *harami*s!" Noora struggled to break free, his legs screeching against the ground as he was dragged away from the scene by Jogi.

Someone in the crowd yelled, "Police, run!" Far in the distance they could hear the whistles blowing and the batons clamoring against the storefront metal shutters.

"Get on your feet and run." Jogi dropped Noora on the ground.

And they ran, in every direction, like an enraged river gushing through a broken dam. They were the children of the streets. They knew the corners, the turns, the secret openings. Each strike of the batons by the police on their backs made them wiser. They lived, and they learned. And the beaten-down paths and cobblestone streets welcomed them with open arms.

Coughing, panting, out of breath, they ended up on the bridge over the dried-out banks of the Ravi River. They slid their way underneath the bridge. Large, cement sewage pipes were laid under the bridge. A quick distant gaze saw nothing but the giant, round openings of those pipes, stretched at least for a couple of miles. They were all dry, reminders of the old plumbing abandoned by the municipality and now occupied by the street children, Jogi told Yosef and Daud.

The front openings of some of those pipes were covered with hand-tied drapery for solitude; others were wide open, the occupants visible to everyone. Some lay there and smoked, some played *Ludo*. There were a few who skimmed through old magazines in the dimmed light of a kerosene lantern, surrounded by salvaged and discarded household items which they must have scavenged. The majority of them gave familiar smiles to Jogi and waved at him. Jogi brought Yosef and Daud to his designated pipe. Daud wondered how everyone remembered which pipe belonged to whom. They all looked the same to him, and there were no markings on any of them. They called the place, "the Ring."

"Its easy." Jogi laughed at Daud's question. "You walk in the wrong ring, you get scolded, or have things thrown at you. After a couple of times, you know exactly where your spot is."

Later that night, lying on a thin twin mattress, Yosef informed Daud what Jogi had told him. He told Daud about the market square four miles south of there, where many of the street urchins went early in the morning looking for work.

"Jogi said he can take us there and help us find work," Yosef said.

Yosef ran through the rules Jogi had laid out: Doing drugs of any kind, *hashish*, *ganja*, sniffing glue, being found in an alley with a needle stuck in one of the arms meant immediate dismissal from the gang. Any trouble with the police, they were not to try to be heroes and should contact Jogi right away. He paid monthly and knew the right people at the police station. Any trip to a brothel, they were to use protection and not bring any diseases back with them.

Daud listened and stared at the arched roof of the pipe. Their bed was set up toward the back of the pipe. Jogi slept at the front. His snoring was loud and erratic. It echoed inside the pipe, making it sound like it was coming from a cave.

Yosef was about to doze off when he heard Daud snivel. He lay there in silence and waited for the sobbing to subside.

"I understand this is too much for you to see and experience in such a short time," Yosef finally turned to Daud and said. Daud burst into tears.

"I don't blame you for being afraid. I am frightened too." Yosef searched for Daud's shoulder in the dark. Daud said something. The words got jumbled up with sniffles and hiccups.

"I am glad you understand what I am saying."

Daud sniffled and mumbled again.

"What's that?" Yosef asked.

"I said, that is not it." Daud cleared his nose and sounded coherent.

"What is it then?"

Daud hesitated.

"In that case, I will turn over and go to sleep. Feel free to cry your heart out all night." Yosef turned over.

"I haven't gone all day!"

"What?"

"I haven't taken a shit. And I don't know where to go now!" Daud's eyes got watery again, and his voice choked.

"Why didn't you say so in the first place?" Yosef grunted. "Let's go outside and find a place where you can squat."

Daud dreamt that night of being again in the bus with Yosef. It was dark outside, and the murky light inside flickered as the bus jumped over the unpaved, rocky road. The bus had gained momentum and was sprinting over the road bumps and sharp bends, making Daud and Yosef bounce off their seat. Daud looked around: There was no one else in the bus except for the driver. The bus spurted through the darkness of the valley, its engine grunting with the increasing pressure on the accelerator.

The wind whistled and howled outside the windows. The next second there was a loud booming sound. The bus jumped up and swiveled violently. Both Yosef and Daud bounced at least a foot off their seat. Moments passed as they remained suspended in the air. It was as if time had stopped in that moment. All sounds were subdued, as if they had gone underwater. And then, just like a flash, it all came back. Daud smashed back to the seat and looked up. Yosef was still suspended in the air, and then some force sucked him toward the back of the bus. He flew in the air with his hands and legs extended outwards. One of the back windows of the bus smashed with tiny round pieces flying all over. In an instant, Yosef was sucked out of that hole, through the broken glass.

Terrified and shaking, Daud raised his head to look at the driver whose back was toward him. What was he supposed to do? How was he to arrive at his destination now that Yosef was gone, the only one who could hold his hand and guide him, protect him from the danger? The thought of being left on his own set up butterflies in his stomach. He wanted to vomit. With all his power, he inched his way toward the driver, who seemed oblivious to what was happening behind him. Daud wanted to ask the driver to stop the bus. Perhaps they could turn around and look for Yosef who had vanished in the black of the night. His fragile little hands held on to the railing for support as he fought the wind and gravity, trying to approach the driver. He finally came up behind the driver. Seemingly unaware of anything else, the driver was humming a song, his hands on the large steering wheel. "In the dark cold night, I will follow the moon to take me to my lover," were the lyrics to the song he murmured.

Daud placed his left hand on the driver's shoulder to gain his attention. The driver slowly turned his head to look at him. Daud's heart sank and pain ran through his stomach. It was as if someone had squeezed his intestines with two iron hands. He threw up all over the windshield. It was Akbar staring at him, driving the bus. His eyes were bloody, and both his hands and feet were limp, dangling, held loosely by the skin. Daud wanted to scream. He opened his mouth, but no sound came out. He wanted to look away, but his terrified gaze was fixed on Akbar, who was motioning him to come closer. Daud retreated, his eyes wide with fear. He ran toward to back of the bus and turned to look. Akbar was now on the bus floor, crawling toward him. Who was driving the bus? Daud thought.

Inside the Ring, Daud lay next to Yosef and dreamt, soaked in sweat, eyes moving rapidly inside closed lids.

4 MINA

August 21, 1999

She heard the buzzing sound coming right above her face. A bee had flown in from the window. It hovered above her face, flapping its wings thousands of times per minute, before landing on her nose. She had spent the rest of the night awake with her eyes closed. The back of her shirt was crusty, dried now after being wet from the sweat and humidity overnight — there was still no electricity. The bee flew away as she turned her head. It was starting to get light outside. Birds had started to chirp. She sat up and touched the floor with her toes. Thinking of Raja, she said a silent prayer. She poured water in a kettle and put it on the stove to make tea. Looking outside through the window into the morning mist, memories started flooding into her mind like pouring rain.

Born on a small farm in a small town called Rampura, far from the city, she had been a little girl who dreamt of fairies, slept listening to fables of princes and kings, and gazed at the stars above, wondering if they were staring back at her. Her parents cultivated fields owned by the tribal chief of the village. In turn, they were given a hut to live in, with a short, rectangular thatched roof. They were also allowed to take in five percent of the cultivated crops. This was a centuries-old tradition. One family, a wealthy one, owned the farms and fields for generations in the entire village. And the generations of peasants worked on the farms for their employers. Hierarchy ran parallel on both sides.

Her parents named her Mina. She had long, black, dusty hair, dark-brown eyes, and dimpled cheeks with a mole on one of them. Mina played in the fields of barley while her parents worked the farm. She ran around, giggling, playing hide and seek with her friends. The warm and gentle breeze flapped her hair in the air as she went higher and higher on a swing. She felt closer to the sky each time she pushed up the swing. She could almost touch the fluffy clouds right above in the blue sky, she thought. She closed her eyes and felt she was floating up on the sky, so free and careless. Mina helped her parents with daily chores after school and brought tea to her father, Khadim Ali, who gathered each evening at the town center with the rest of the peasants for gossip and daily news. At night, Mina lay in the veranda facing the glittering stars in the infinite black of the sky. Holding a plastic doll, the only toy she had, she dreamt of being a princess one day, because that is what her mother told her she was.

One cool fall evening, Mina grabbed the thermos of hot tea and walked up her usual route to the town square to give her father tea. The pale gold of the fading sun sprinkled across the green field. Young boys playing soccer on the far end of a field made occasional shrieking noise. Mina, fourteen, walked the familiar streets of the town on her way to the town square. It was the usual crowd. Most of them were familiar faces she had grown up seeing. Some nodded as she passed, others accepted the "*salam*" she offered. She made her way through the crowd, nodding and smiling to people around her, on her way to greet her father. Her eyes became fixed on a face, a strange one. She had never seen him before. He was tall and wore a white dress. The number of gold rings on his fingers and chains on the neck indicated his well-to-do status. He was lean, with a big nose that sat right above his trim moustache. His round, black eyes were pushed back, but his gaze was sharp and prominent. He sat on a high chair, fixated on Mina. She flushed, suddenly embarrassed by the feeling that a pair of eyes were crawling over every inch of her body. Mina felt intimidated and uncomfortable by his gaze.

"He is the chief's brother and lives in the city," Mina's father told her over dinner that night. "He wants to take over some of the land to build a factory."

"Hum," she said.

"What does that mean?"

"I did not like him," said Mina.

"Why do you say that? You don't even know the man!"

"I did not like the way he sat high, separate from rest of the crowd, as if he were better than every one else." Mina had annoyance in her tone.

"He owns the land in this village. He is better than the rest of us. He is the owner and he does sit high, above the peasants," her father snapped. "God forbid, child! Don't speak evil of someone who never crossed your path before." Mina picked up the plates when they finished dinner. She did not mention how her heart had pounded against her chest when she had seen him looking at her.

Three weeks later, her father stormed into the house, panting, almost knocking over the water pitcher. He grabbed his wife by the elbow and dragged her in the other room where Mina lay.

"Out of the room!" her father exclaimed.

"What happened?"

"I said leave, now!"

Not sure of what was going on, Mina tried to listen in, but was prevented by the locked door. She heard her parents talking in loud voices. Her heart raced as she pressed her ears against the door and tried to listen. She heard her mother crying and her father's footsteps frantically pacing back and forth.

That night, her mother whispered in her ears, "You are not to leave the house alone again."

Shocked by the news, Mina looked into her mother's face, her big black eyes puzzled and carrying the question, "What did I do?"

"And what is your business walking down the street scantly clad?" Her mother slapped her on the face.

Stunned, Mina put her hand on the reddened cheek but didn't say anything. She didn't try to stop the tears that rolled down her face.

"You have to cover your head from now on, do you hear me?" Her mother's voice was choking. "They all gossiped that giving birth to a daughter was nothing but liability. Little did I know, fourteen years later, their argument would turn into reality."

Mina placed her hand on her mother's.

"Your father will make the arrangements to send you off to live with your grandmother for a while." Her mother ran her fingers through Mina's long black hair.

Mina did not sleep that night. She had questions, but she did not ask. A liability, a burden. Her existence suddenly seemed so meaningless. She pictured her father secretly praying for a boy when she was being born. And she could see the look of disappointment when he saw her for the first time. The guilt of being a girl cut deep through her chest. How she wished her father to be proud of his child, a girl.

The night before her departure, Mina's mother made her favorite dish, *saag paneer* (spinach and goat cheese) and corn bread.

Mina watched her mother roll flour and water into dough and then into flatbread before cooking it on top of the kerosene stove. They sat around the blue and yellow flames of the stove and ate dinner, quietly.

Mina could not put the food down her throat. She was being sent off to a different town to live with her grandmother. She did not know when she would be coming back. She did not want to leave.

"Eat, *bacha*, this is your favorite dish." Mina's father put his hand on her head when he saw her sad and pale face.

"You never told me why you wanted to get rid of me." She sounded angry.

"No one wants to get rid of you. You are all we have in our lives. You are not safe here. Once things get settled down, we will unite again, I promise." Her father hugged her.

Mina listened to dogs and coyotes barking outside while she took out clean clothes to wear in the morning, pink trousers and a white *kameez* with matching pink embroidery around the neck. An unforeseen and unpredictable future awaited her when she would get on the bus in the morning to go live with her grandmother. Something was not right, she could feel it. Why would her parents so forcefully send her away all of a sudden, so quickly and hastily? She could not comprehend. Nobody would tell her anything. Mina felt angry and helpless. Her mind kept wandering into her imagination and thoughts of the unknown till her eyelids got heavy. She lay down on the cot, and her thoughts faded into dreams. She dreamt of the fields, the streets, the playground in her backyard. It was all empty. She was the only one in the town, running between streets. Everyone seemed to have left their business unattended and vanished. She called for her friends, but did not hear a reply. She kept running. Her heart was pounding, and all of sudden the land ended underneath her. It was nothing but a deep void down below, and she was falling into it. She felt cold. Her heart dropped as she felt butterflies in her stomach. She was going down rapidly, and there was no one to save her. And then she heard a loud banging noise.

She woke up from her dream, soaking wet in her sweat, and laid motionless for a while. She heard the same sound again. Oh God, it's the neighbor's cat again, trying to climb up the pots in the kitchen, she thought, and decided to go up to the veranda to shoo her off. As she started to get up, the door slammed open and three men entered the room. Their faces were covered, and they were carrying guns. Mina let out a shriek, and she heard her father running toward the room. One of the men approached her and put his hands on her mouth before she could let out another scream. He wrapped his other arm around her and lifted her with a firm grip. Mina tried helplessly to flee from the man's arm, but was no match to his strong power. Her father rushed into the room and attacked one of the other two men with an axe. The man skillfully dodged the flying axe and smashed her father's head with his pistol's handle. Blood gushed out of his forehead, and he slumped to the floor.

"Get the girl and go!" the third man said to the others.

They grabbed Mina and headed for the main door. Her mother came screaming from the corner and attacked one of the men with a piece of lumber. One man snatched the stick from her hands and pushed her aside. Unable to keep her balance, Mina's mother fell down to the ground. She cried and howled at the men taking her daughter away. By that time, all three men were in the Jeep they had come in. They stuffed Mina in the back end of the vehicle and drove off amid the watching neighbors, who had gathered outside their houses after listening to all the shouting.

Mina opened her eyes. It was a low-ceilinged room with grey color painted on the walls. She lay motionless for few seconds. Her head spun, her heart beat a millions beat per second. She took deep breaths and rested her head flat on the bed. Gradually, memories of what had happened started rushing into her mind. Her eyes widened. Images of her father covered in blood and her mother dropped on the ground, weeping, crying, shouting, ran through her mind. She looked around and saw four images through her blurry vision. A cold wind swept through her, and she realized she was undressed. Mina moved her arms to wrap around her chest. Her hands were tied to the bed. She frantically jerked around to free herself, fighting the tears of helplessness streaming down her checks. She saw the images moving closer. Three of them were the same men who had abducted her. And the fourth one was a familiar face she had seen before. He was the man she had seen at the town square wearing white clothes, the chief's brother. His eyes were fixed on Mina's face. Mina felt his piercing eyes penetrating through her body. He leaned over her and his lips parted, spreading a smirk on his face.

"At last, we meet," he said. "This is not how I envisioned it, though."

"Please let me get back to my parents," Mina pleaded.

"When this is over, you can blame your father for this."

"I have done no wrong to you. I don't even know you!" she cried.

"I asked your father for your hand for *mut'ah* (temporary marriage), but he refused. He called it legalized prostitution." His hands were now resting on Mina's ankle. "He should have been honored that I asked for your hand as an honorable man, according to the law. But he refused." He sighed. "I don't take no for an answer very well, my little *bulbul* (nightingale)." Mina felt his fingers crawling up. She winced at the thought of it. "Trying to sneak you out of the village was not a smart move." Mina felt the steam of his reeking breath on her cheek. "So blame him for this night, my *bulbul*."

Mina knew the bus would leave the station without her. She would never make it to her grandmother's house. Her mother and father would not be visiting her at the end of each season's change. She witnessed her dreams of one day being a princess shattered as those men approached her. Throughout the night, she cried and screamed. But all she heard in return was laughter that echoed in the room. At times, her throat, cracked due to constant screaming, made no sound. Then she saw images of her parents.

"I wish I hadn't given birth to you!" her mother cried, standing at the corner.

"I should have buried you alive, so I didn't have to see this day." her father sneered, pointing his finger at her.

"How are we going to walk the streets with our heads up high?" Her mother slapped her chest.

"You brought nothing but shame and dishonor to this family!" she heard her father exclaim.

"Liability, burden, shame, disgrace!" Those words resonated around her.

Her attackers drank, danced around her, punched her in the face, kicked her, poured alcohol on her body, and took turns raping her.

By morning, Mina was a mere piece of flesh, bruised, wounded, bleeding, barely conscious. The assault stopped only after her attackers were so intoxicated by drinking heavily all night that they passed out.

Later that day, at the police station four miles south of the village, sat Kashif, the chief's brother, red-eyed and hung-over. He had been escorted to the superintendent's office and offered tea and pastries. Right outside the office, further down the hall, on a wooden bench, Khadim Ali sat. His head was covered in white bandage. His eyes were puffy and red from being up all night and crying. He had been sitting there for hours now, waiting to be heard.

Ultimately, the superintendent nodded at the constable, and Khadim Ali was ushered in. Weak from the assault and mentally exhausted from the previous evening, he walked in with tired steps and plummeted onto the chair in front of the superintendent.

"Who took care of your head?" The superintendent pointed at the bandage. Khadim ran his hand over the bandage. His eyes were fixed on the floor.

"Khadim Ali?"

"My wife fixed it for me. She helped me stop the bleeding." he finally answered.

"Why don't you tell us what happened last night?" the superintendent asked.

"Four men broke into my house last night. They attacked me and kidnapped my daughter. I cannot find her." His voice choked before breaking into tears.

"Did you identify the intruders?"

Khadim said that he had not seen them before.

"But I know who sent them!" Khadim Ali slightly tilted his head toward Kashif.

The superintendent, a thick and beefy man in a gray and khaki uniform, walked from behind the desk and sat at the edge of it, next to Khadim. He exchanged glances with Kashif.

"It is a grave tragedy. Being the father of two daughters, I can sympathize." The superintendent placed his hands on Mina's father's shoulders. "Who do you think sent those men to your house?"

"This man." Mina's father pointed his finger toward Kashif.

"Are you sure?"

"Yes!"

"I can see how you can be stressed after what might have happened in your house." The superintendent cleared his throat. "But this is a serious allegation. I ask that you be very careful before accusing someone of kidnapping your daughter."

Kashif sat across from both of them and pretended not to notice his name being brought up in the conversation.

"He—this man—" Khadim Ali pointed at Kashif, "asked if I would give Mina's hand to him under *mut'ah*. In exchange he offered me money."

"And what did you say to that?"

"I refused."

"How long ago was it?"

"About three weeks ago. I refused and told him that she was not to be someone's temporary wife to be sent back when he was done with her," Khadim Ali said.

"Go on," the superintendent nodded.

"She was to leave last night to go live with her grandmother. His men stormed into my house and took her." Khadim's voice choked again. "I want to know if my daughter is safe and alive."

The superintendent looked at Kashif and paused for few seconds as if trying to find the right words for what he was about to say.

"Your daughter is alive," he finally said.

Khadim's eyes brightened as he sat back up with the news. "Please take me to her. I want to see and bring my daughter back."

"It's best that you don't see her and that she does not come back!" the superintendent said in a low voice.

"Why?"

"Your story doesn't correlate with what I have heard from Kashif."

"What?! I am telling the truth!"

"Based on what I have heard, your daughter has been secretly seeing this man for several weeks now. She left the house last night of her own consent and spent the night with four men willingly."

"That is a lie," Khadim Ali screamed.

"Nothing is proven, but I am telling you what I have heard from the other party."

"It is not true!" Khadim cupped his face. "My Mina will never do such a thing."

"Your daughter left home. She spent the night with four men. Need I say more to you? She is not honorable enough to come back to you, or the village."

Within seconds, the circles under Khadim's eyes grew darker, and his hair dropped from his head like leaves from an autumn tree. With life quickly fading from his eyes, in those few moments he grew a decade older.

"Do you understand now?" The superintendent looked at Khadim's face that had suddenly turned pale.

"I ... I ... my daughter has been victimized. I want to file a complaint and have the assailants arrested!"

"Have you thought about it fully?" the superintendent responded.

"What is there to think about? My daughter is innocent. This man ruined her life!" Khadim Ali shouted.

"I'll be more than happy to file the report for you. I can see you are hurt, and that is understandable for what you went through," the superintendent said. "Did four adult males witness the assault?"

"What are you talking about?" Khadim Ali frowned.

"Can you produce four males who can testify that they saw your daughter being raped by those men last night?" the superintendent asked again.

"My daughter was kidnapped and taken to an unknown location! How and where would I find four witnesses who saw the crime?"

"Then you know the law, the '*Hudood* law.' The superintendent sat back in his swivel chair. "According to the law, if you file the complaint for rape, you need to produce four adult males who witnessed the crime taking place. If you can't, your daughter will be tried for adultery. The lack of witnesses will imply that she had consensual sex with those men and that she committed adultery. She will be imprisoned for her crime." The superintendent leaned forward, his eyebrows raised. "Do you want this burden to be heavier than it already is?"

"What about my neighbors who saw Mina being kidnapped by those men?" Khadim Ali asked.

"That is not for you to worry about. No one will say anything as long as you keep your mouth shut."

"I would like to see my daughter," Khadim Ali pleaded.

"Soon, my friend. Be patient a little longer," the superintendent said. "Just remember, your next visit to her will be your last. Prepare for that. Your daughter goes with Kashif to the city."

Mina's parents were driven to an old, pale-brick house where they saw Mina for the last time. The house stood in the middle of deep woods along an unpaved dirt road which snaked its way mile after mile further inland. Both father and mother were ushered to a room at the far end of the house. There, on a single bed on a muddy sheet and blanket, sat Mina, silent and still. She covered herself with the blanket as she saw her parents enter.

Her mother, shatter-hearted and soaked in tears, slowly approached her and held her hand. She turned Mina's face and saw the blackened bruises on her face and let out a cry.

Mina wore a man's shirt and long, tattered pants instead of the clothes she had worn when she was kidnapped. Her father buried his eyes under his thumb and index finger.

"*Baba!*" Mina called for her father.

"My child!" her mother wept.

"They said ..." Khadim Ali began.

"What?" Mina asked.

"Don't talk." Mina's mother tried to stop her husband.

"Did you, *bacha*?" Khadim Ali asked.

"*Baba*, please speak!" Mina yelped.

"Let her be," her mother decreed.

"They said you left the house willingly."

And there it was: the burden, guilt, shame, and doubt, Mina thought, that she had brought with her the day she opened her eyes to the world. She lowered her head.

"Say no more, my child." Her mother placed her hands on Mina's lips.

"Kashif told me to blame you, father, for what happened to me." Mina said in a lower voice. "To blame you."

Mina never saw her parents again and was sent to live in the city and marry one of the servants who worked for Kashif.

. . .

The high-pitched gurgling sound of boiling water brought Mina out of the murky clouds of memories. She caught a glimpse of her reflection in the mirror. Her fingers ran over her face. Counting the years back told her she would be turning thirty soon. The image in front of her told a different story. Aged scars, battered lines running across her forehead and temples, and strands of white hair shimmering against the sunlight indicated time had not been too kind to her.

She gazed outside the window while sipping tea. It had been a year since her first husband died. He was a good man, a cobbler. He never questioned the validity of her giving birth to Saif seven months into the marriage. Six months after his death, Kashif matched her up with another man, unemployed and an alcoholic.

There was a knock on the door which broke her chain of thoughts. She opened the door and saw Saif standing outside.

Mina ushered him in and asked if he would like some tea and *roti*.

"Is he around?" Saif asked.

"You don't have to worry about him."

"I worry about you being around him." Saif followed his mother into the kitchen.

"He is sound asleep and will not bother us," Mina said.

"Came home late, I suppose, drunk?"

"Let's have some breakfast together, you and me," Mina tried to change the subject. "Where is Raja?"

Saif recalled going back to the house late after dark to see if Raja was still at the job.

"I have not seen him since yesterday morning. And I wonder if he came to see you." Saif placed his weight on the kitchen counter and shifted sideways, balancing on his elbow.

"What do you mean? I have not seen him since the day he left here." Mina stared at Saif.

"I thought he came here after the job yesterday." Saif ran his fingers through his hair and started to pace back and forth.

"What job?" Mina asked. Her heart started beating at the unusual rate she had felt the night before. Saif recounted yesterday morning to her, about Raja's first job.

"Did you go back to the job site to look for him?" Mina asked.

"I did, late in the evening, just to make sure Raja had left from there."

"And?" Mina asked.

"There was no answer. It was dark, and there were no lights coming out of the house. I knocked several times on the door, but no one came out"

"Where do you think he went? I mean ... you are on the streets with him. You would know if there are any hideouts, a friend he may have gone to see?" Mina asked, looking into Saif's eyes, hoping to get the response she was looking for.

Saif thought about searching for his brother last night at park benches, train station platforms, shelters, graveyards. He had even scoured dark alleys, uncovering the heads of some who sat there and sniffed glue.

"It is possible that he might have stayed overnight with some friend," Saif responded. He saw the concerned look on Mina's face. "He is probably back by now." He could not find the courage to tell her that he had looked for Raja a good part of last night, but he was nowhere to be found.

"Find him, son, and tell him his mother is worried sick about him."

They heard coughing and a groggy sound coming from the other room. Her husband was waking up.

"Raja will turn up soon, *amma*. Soon," Saif said, and left.

. . .

October 14, 1999

Shadows crept into the city as the smog-filled dusk approached. The fleeting yellow of the sun mixed in with the gray exhaust fumes made everything look fuzzy. Saif stood at a busy intersection on Mall Road. A batch of cars stopped at the red light. He limped his way toward the middle of the intersection holding a bucket and squeegee and started cleaning the windshields of cars in the front row. He had timing of the traffic light down to a science: In an average forty-five to sixty-second interval Saif could wet, squeegee clean, and rag dry close to ten cars. Although some cars took off without paying him, he was able to collect between ten and fifteen rupees at each red light. He shared the intersection with another boy, who worked from morning till afternoon. Certain city corners, the busy ones, were designated and leased on a monthly basis to street children by their gang leaders.

Saif straightened the last curled-up bill in his pocket and decided it was time to quit for the day. The lamp above him cranked and a wimpy, yellow light started to flicker. He heard his name being called from across the street. As he looked up, he saw another boy from Jogi's gang riding by on a bicycle.

"Go see your mother!" the boy in the cycle exclaimed.

"What?"

A crowded, loud bus passed through the intersection. Black smoke from the exhaust darkened the view. Coughing, Saif waved the smoke away with his arms.

"Your *amma*. She is harassing every boy she can find on the street, asking for you. Go see her and tell her not everyone on the street knows where you live." The boy delivered the message without fully stopping the bicycle and rode away.

Saif had not been back to see his mother. He knew she was looking for him. He received most of the messages she sent to him through strangers. He had not seen her since the day after Raja disappeared, close to two months ago. He could not stand the thought of seeing the dying glimmer of hope in her eyes if she saw him. Her gaze would rekindle on seeing him, he knew, hoping he had brought news about his younger brother. But he had no news about Raja. In reality, he was not sure how to tell his mother that Raja wasn't the only child living on the street who had vanished.

It was the way of life for a lot of the street children. Some of them moved to different locations or even cities. Others found a reason to stay off the street. It wasn't unusual for an urchin to pack his belongings overnight and disappear. Their neighbors at the Ring, upon finding an empty sewage pipe the next day, discussed the missing for a few days before taking them off their minds. At times the ones who had left showed up at Café Pyala, bringing gossip and tales of their journeys.

September 16, 1999

Jogi stood and stared at the empty pipes. Uninhabited pipes meant lost rent and less money to pay monthly to the police. They will chew up my ass when I show up this month, he thought. He rubbed his arms as a cold wind blew from the river. All these years on the street, he had never seen so many street children vanish during such a short amount of time. Accounts of some of the children being hired for labor at the market square and not returning had him puzzled all the more. He thought of Saif, who claimed that his young brother, the latest of the missing urchins, left with three men for work and had not returned.

"My brother has gone missing, *dada*." Jogi recalled his conversation with Saif a few weeks ago.

Jogi and Yosef were sitting at Café Pyala when Saif had walked in. It was an early fall afternoon. Several inches of rain from two days ago had left the space saturated with humidity and no air movement. The westward sunlight peeked from the window and filtered through Jogi's hair. Dust particles struggled to stay afloat in a thick, wet, heavy air mass. The ceiling fan above made clicking noise.

"He left for work two days ago. I have not seen him since," Saif's voice choked.

Jogi glanced over at Yosef and leaned over at the table.

"Tell me."

Standing in front of so many vacant sewage pipes, Jogi wondered what had happened to its occupants. Saif's account about Raja being picked up for work and not returning echoed in Jogi's ears.

At Café Pyala, later that evening, a busy crowd hustled to get as close to the front as possible. They all looked at Jogi, who sat at the front. The room buzzed with snippets. Not everyone knew why a meeting was called on such a short notice.

"How many?" Jogi asked the boy standing against the wall. He was sitting backwards on a chair with his chest pressed against the chair's back.

"Thirty-eight," the boy did a final count under his breath and announced. He was a petite boy with emerald green eyes, dark hair, and thin eyebrows; he wore a green, long shirt with the hem touching his knees, and black slacks with flat bottoms.

Jogi glanced across the crowd of street urchins gathered. Thirty-eight boys from his gang had disappeared over the course of six months. He straightened up and cleared his throat.

"I wouldn't usually be this cautious, but we have thirty-eight among us who have disappeared," Jogi said loudly to the crowd. Many turned to look at each other.

"The number is alarming because all thirty-eight of them left within the last six months. How many among you know of someone who has disappeared during the last six months?"

Several among them started to rise, one by one, slowly. Before Jogi's eyes, there were soon fifteen boys standing, including Saif and Yosef, claiming to have lost someone they knew in the gang. Jogi gasped. Had he failed to protect his gang from the danger lurking out on the street, he wondered.

"How many, of the missing you know, frequently went to the market square to look for work?" Jogi's heart pounded when he asked that question.

Fourteen out of fifteen standing raised their hands.

"Our gang isn't the only one," someone from the back of the crowd shouted. All heads turned in that direction. "Other gangs across town have reported some missing in their group too," said a boy with curly hair on a perfectly round head, who stood up toward the back of the crowd.

"What is going on?" someone else in the crowded yelled. Jogi could feel the situation turning riotous. But this was not the time to try to tame the crowd. There was no easy way to do this:

"I want all of you to stay away from the market square. Stay in groups at all times, and do not take any job past sunset," he declared.

'What—" "Why—" "Who—" echoed from different directions. A dense buzzing sound filled the air. Words became garbled and fuzzy.

"Who is after us?" someone shouted at the top of his lungs. Jogi heard a plate shattering on the floor. From the corner of his eye he saw two boys pushing each other. With lightning speed, Jogi's hands pierced between their chests and separated them before it could turn into a brawl. He stood on a chair.

"Listen to me, and listen good. You want to live, you pay attention to my words." Like a tsunami, his deep, commanding voice swept across the room. "You have trusted me before. And I ask you do the same one more time. It could be nothing, and all thirty-eight of our gang have probably moved on. I hope tomorrow you will come up to my face and tell me how wrong I was being so cautious." Jogi paused to take a look. He had their undivided attention. "But until I know for sure, as your leader, you do what I ask of you. No one is after you." He sounded convincing, although he was not sure of his own words. "Give me time to find why so many among us have left."

That calmed the rowdy crowd, and it dispersed. Some boys danced and chanted Jogi's name in praise.

After the meeting, long after the café's clay oven was put out, the dishes went through their final wash for the night, and the café owner did a final tally at the cash register, Saif sat right across from Jogi, absently shuffling through a deck of cards. On other nights Saif enjoyed this hangout as it buzzed with laughter, chatter, bets being placed on a game of bluff, the clunking sound of cutlery being moved around, and music playing through loudspeakers. That night he needed it to be quiet, very still. He silently wished for sleep to come that night, unlike several nights in the past when he closed his eyes and thought of the moment he saw Raja last. He slowly got up and limped over to grab his walking cane. People at the shelter had given him a donated cane to help him walk better.

"You are not losing hope. Tell me you are not." Jogi placed his hands on Saif's shoulder as he turned to walk out.

"How can I lose something I did not have in the first place?" Saif offered a weak smile.

"I am hopeful," Jogi said.

Saif's fingers gripped the handle of the rustic cane. His arm trembled as he tried to balance himself on it. "Then go and put your hope to some good use. You are lucky you have it."

"I want to know if you have faith in me."

"If faith can feed me for a day, save me from being picked up by the police, and bring back my brother, then yes: I have all the faith in the world."

Jogi placed his hand on Saif's shaking hand holding the cane. "Don't give up, not just yet."

. . .

Late October brought miasma and fog in the evening air, creating a halo around the street lamps. Saif walked along the sidewalk aimlessly for a while. He walked on McLeod Road, past St. Andrew Church and on to Bohr Wala Chowk. The message had been received. *Amma* was looking for him. She wanted to know why Raja had not come back home for two months. He found himself standing outside the railway station. It was where he had brought Raja the night he had left home and come to live with him. Raja stood on the platform, Saif recalled, holding his brother's fingers, mesmerized. A steam locomotive approaching the station had fascinated him. Raja had jumped and clapped his hands as the whistling sound of steam erupted from the engine. The sound of his brother's clap echoed away into the haunted night. There was no steam engine roaring into the station that October night. Saif stood alone on the dark, deserted platform.

As he stepped back, hurriedly, trying to walk out of the platform, his cane got stuck in the cracked cement on the platform floor. He grabbed the cane and broke it in two in frustration, tossing it to the side, his hands shaking helplessly. Saif remembered going back to the house on Ravi Road many times, looking for Raja. He even returned to the market square several times to see if the three men were back soliciting labor. Sometimes he knocked on the house door and got no answer. Other times he simply hovered around and stared at the walls that had swallowed his young brother. A couple of times he was spotted by the local gang in the neighborhood, who shoved him around and mocked him when he limped and tried to get away. His feet started heading once again in the direction of Ravi Road. Strangely, the thought of being by the house gave him comfort. He could not think of another place that would bring balm to his wounded heart.

He remembered walking through the streets to get to the house when those men had hired Raja. Saif had gone with them so he could see where Raja was working. The house was situated in one of the most congested parts of the old town. Just like the rest of the city, the neighborhood was inherited from the British occupation more than sixty years ago, cutting across the Ravi River. Not much had changed since then. The entire neighborhood was a cluster of adjacent, two-story brick houses built by Hindus living there before the India–Pakistan separation in 1947. The buildings lined both sides of narrow cobblestone streets, with storefronts on the ground floor. There was space for only one car to pass through at any given time. The majority of people rode motorcycles or Vespas. Being below the Ravi River delta, the neighborhood was sunk below ground level. The sun never got around to shining more than a few rays on the neighborhood, due to the low ground and the surrounding multistory buildings facing each other only a few feet apart, blocking the sunlight. Most of the houses had a plastered façade. Some broke tradition and had stone-front walls. Political and marketing banners hung in the air, high above the ground, tied from the wrought iron balconies of houses on each end of the streets.

Saif turned street corners as he had several times before. He had memorized certain landmarks to keep him on the right course: the produce shop at the corner of the first turn, the color-dyeing factory at the end of the second street, and the butcher shop four stores before the following left turn. Following his self-taught directions, Saif ended up in front of the house. That was the only house on the street that was not multistory. His heart started beating faster, as it had on his previous visits.

The front of the house was secured by a black iron gate with spikes on top. Saif remembered that the door opened into a courtyard leading to two rooms. He had wanted to peek into it the day he dropped off Raja, but was shooed off by the men.

"Move along! Come back in the evening to pick him up." One of the men stretched his arm and pointed at the main road.

Saif inquired of a passerby about the hour of the day. He seemed to have lost the concept of time. Once told it was past ten, he looked around and realized it was night. He pushed his back against the wall across from the house and waited. Half an hour later, the street was virtually deserted.

Fairly confident he wouldn't be disturbed, Saif edged toward the house and pressed his ear against the gate. The cold metal against his skin sent shivers down his spine. In his heart, he wished Raja would call out his name from inside. Or perhaps one of the men would open the gate and usher Raja out, saying, "Look, he has been hiding here all this time. Go, *bacha*, your brother is here to pick you up. So long!"

There was no sound coming through the gate. The color of the night was changing from amber to blue to purple, each shade getting darker with each passing minute. There was no light on to illuminate the inside of the house. Saif took one more look around. There was no sign of any gang approaching. He reshifted his attention back to the house. The right wall of the house was separated from the next house by a little over twelve inches, he noticed. He walked toward the narrow opening and looked up at the walls. There was a transom high up on the wall to his left, fortified by vertical iron bars. Gingerly Saif inserted himself sideways into the opening, his chest a few inches from one wall, his back almost touching the other. He tilted his head and looked up again. There was a cement ledge right outside the transom that, once reached, could be held on to.

The walls of both houses were close enough to climb up perpendicularly with both feet. Saif turned and faced the street. He placed both hands on each wall. Next he slipped his shoes off and placed his right foot on the wall below his right hand. Applying firm pressure through his left leg, he pulled his body upward and lifted himself in the air, then firmly secured his left foot on the wall. Saif was now standing in the air, inches off the ground. His hands and feet gripped the cold, grainy cement walls on both sides, like a lizard. By shifting his hands up the wall and then his feet, Saif raised his body up and crawled up slowly, continually repositioning his feet and hands against the walls. Small beads of sweat broke through his pores. The skin on his hands and feet turned red, caused by the friction against the concrete.

He wondered what awaited him once he reached the transom and looked inside. Did Raja work in that room? Will I find him tied to a bed in there? I will call out his name, maybe toss a little piece of rock at him to wake him up. Will I call the police? What about the warnings from Jogi on steering clear of the police? His brain worked as hard as his arms and legs. He paused halfway up, caught his breath, and took one look down. He was alone. He started inching his way up again toward the transom with his hands and feet. His face muscles contracted as he squinted and winced with each step, moving against gravity. Taking calculated steps, Saif reached the transom. He pressed his weight against the wall on his left and leaped to grab the iron bars of the transom with both hands. After a minor readjustment, Saif dangled on the wall, his legs suspended in the air, his hands quivering as he clutched the wrought-iron bars. He looked inside.

It was black. His eyes wandered through the dark inside the room without much success. The vista in front of his eyes was murky. The only thing he could make out was that it was a high-ceilinged room with an unlit bulb hanging down from that ceiling. Saif slowly reached into his pocket with his right hand. His muscles stretched as his entire body weight shifted to his left hand. Grimacing and panting, he took out a piece of folded paper and a small lighter. It was the back page of a magazine where he had seen a picture of a female model and torn the page off. The longing of fantasizing in the Ring about the model was overtaken by the need of lighting it and trying to see inside the room.

Suspended by one hand, Saif blew air across his face by extending his lower lip outwards. The resulting upward air hit the target and shifted the perspiration bursting out of his pores and eyebrows, moving it onto the side of his face instead of having it drop into his eyes. Next he secured the lighter inside the fist of his left hand as it gripped the transom. Holding the paper in his right hand, Saif arched it toward the lighter and brought it closer. Very carefully, he tried to grind the wheel of the lighter and light the paper. He was well aware that any slight misjudgment would cause his hand to slip, plunging him down, where he was sure break many bones, or even die.

Sparks flew and the lighter ignited at the second attempt, torching the rolled-up paper in Saif's hand. He slid the paper torch through the iron bars of the transom. Flickering, pale firelight speckled on the inside walls of the room, making it dimly lit. Saif waved the burning paper through the air of the room, as the paper swiftly curled into black ashes with red edges. The irises in his eyes squinted to squeeze in as much light as possible. The room appeared empty and the entrance door was closed.

There was no sign of anyone inside. Saif scanned the area. The front wall, in bleak light, seemed dark and dotted all across. His energy was running out rapidly, like the engulfed paper in his hands. After gathering the last bit of his strength, Saif heaved up, pushing against the transom bar to see the room below. Like a gymnast, his body straightened as he balanced his weight on his arms. Through the iridescent flames, his eyes gazed around the room below one more time. He saw a *charpoy* against the side wall, and a chair and side table next to the bed. Other than that, the room appeared empty in the visible light.

Then Saif's eyes rested on what, in that very instant, sank his heart. He tightened his grip on the iron bars as he tried to get a little better look, his cheeks pressed against the wrought iron. All his fears came rushing in, drowning any tiny flare of hope that may have been left in his heart. There, in front of his eyes, were mounds of clothes lying on the floor, piled on top of each other. Sleeves, shirt necks, jerseys, pants, jackets, and hats were layered on top of each other as if ready to be rummaged through by eager customers at a discount clothing store. Another pile next to it consisted of shoes of all kinds: slippers, cruddy gym shoes, flippers — all stuffed in that pile. And there, amid that pile, Saif saw a glistening metal object lying on top of a pair of pants.

He recognized both items. The shiny metal was the bracelet which he had given to Raja, and it lay on top of the pair of pants his brother had worn the morning he came to this house. Burning flames snaked toward his fingers now. Saif tried to take one more peek in hope of seeing more before he had to toss the dying torch onto the street.

Suddenly his body jerked and plunged downwards. Saif felt the blood rushing through his arms as his fingers tightened their grip around the bars at the last second. He felt his left ankle roped around by an iron fist, squeezing into his bones, tugging him down. Dangling, swaying, clutching the transom bars with one hand, Saif looked down. From the dark alley, two eyes were staring up at him.

The hand clutching his ankle tugged at Saif, motioning him to come down. The heat of burning paper lunged toward his fingers. He cringed at the sudden pain and let go of the last of the torch, which disintegrated into ash and vanished in the black of the night. There was no way further up, only down. Saif began lowering himself, indicating to the man standing below that he was coming down voluntarily. The man waited for Saif to descend before grabbing him by the collar and dragging him out of the alley. He slammed Saif against the wall.

"Who are you?" the man asked, his voice low and husky.

He appeared to be in his late forties, with black hair mixed in with gray, a days-old stubble, a faded scar line running from his nose down to the left cheek, his deep-set narrow brown eyes fixed on Saif's face. His thick, hairy arm clutched Saif by the neck.

"Start talking soon. You have caught me at the very lowest of my patience."

He wet the edges of his goatee couple of times with his tongue. Steam coming from his nostrils landed right on Saif's neck.

"I came here looking for someone," Saif squeaked.

"I have seen you circling this house before."

"I told you, I was looking for someone."

"Looking for someone in the dark of the night?" He twisted Saif's collar. "Do you think I was raised by donkeys? Are you one of them?"

"One of who?"

"All the boys who used to come to this house."

"My brother was one of those boys."

"What was your brother doing here?"

"He was brought here for day labor. He never returned," Saif explained.

The shades of doubt in the man's eyes changed, and his grip softened.

The man asked if Saif had seen anything inside through the transom. He let go of Saif, who put his shoes back on.

"I could not see anything inside. It was dark." Saif did not want to share with a stranger that he might have seen Raja's belongings lying on the floor.

The man walked up to a street light and became more visible. He was wearing hooded black sweatshirt. "I thought you were one of them."

"Can you tell me anything about the people who live here?" Saif asked, walking up to him guardedly.

"No one has come in and out of this house in a while," he responded, almost mumbling to himself. "As for those who lived here, nobody knew them. We just knew that they lived here." The man turned and faced Saif. "Have you contacted the police?"

"What?"

"A report about your missing brother — police should have a filed report."

"I ... don't—"

"I understand." The man ran his fingers through the goatee. "No one knew who lived in the house. There were numerous sightings of a man entering and leaving the house, sometime alone, sometime not. No one saw him socialize with anyone in the neighborhood. Rumor has it he was kicked out of the previous neighborhood." The man pointed toward a cement bench nearby and took a seat.

"Sometimes there would be several of them, and at times the house remained dark for days. Nobody knew when they came and left." Saif took a seat right next to the man.

"Did you ever get a look at any of them?"

"Yes, a couple of times late at night when I came home from my night shift. I ran into a young boy, about your age, with a long scar on his left cheek, similar to mine." Saif knew who he was talking about.

"And one time, I saw a man who appeared to be older than the others." man continued.

"The same man you heard was evicted from his old neighborhood?"

"I think so."

"How did you come across him?"

"He was dispensing a dark, oily mixture down the gutters. He looked up at me and offered a smile. To this day, I remember the menace speckled on his face. It was as if I was face to face with the devil." The man's body literally shivered with the thought.

"What did you see?" Saif asked.

"Anger, a soul that had gone to the very depths of hell and come back." The man recited a quick verse from the Quran under his breath. "That man was cursed."

"The entire street and plumbing stank for days. We could not walk on the street for weeks without covering our noses. Neighbors filed a complaint with the city council. I did not see him after that."

"Nobody interacted with them?"

"Aren't you listening? The man and the people who visited him weren't exactly your typical friendly neighbor types." After a pause, the man spoke again. "I hope your brother is out there, somewhere."

Saif accepted the sympathy and started walking again, his limp more prominent due to climbing up the wall. He lost track of which way to go: Jogi? *Amma*? The police? He tried to control his heavy breathing and leaned against a closed door after he turned the corner into another street. He closed his eyes. One thing was for sure: Raja was not coming back of his own accord. Saif fought the urge to think of the alternative. His facial expression tightened. His eyes remained closed. Imagining Raja dead sent shivers down his throat. He felt his breathing pipe closing. He gasped for air as he opened his eyes. And then he hobbled down the empty street, with his crippled leg, as fast as he could.

5 DAUD

June 1998 – July 1999

"*Nawa aya ain sohneya* (You must be new in town, my dear)," Noori Nutt's thunderous voice roared. What followed was a full-throated, verbal brawl. The audience watched in awe as the plot unfolded. The cinema was packed to its capacity. Within the audience sat Yosef, Daud, and Jogi, hunched down in the back row. They had tried the front seats, but been shooed off to the back by the nearby crowd.

"You will love this film," Jogi had proclaimed on the way to the cinema.

The cold winter of Lahore was a distant memory and was replaced with sweltering June weather. Now into their fourth month in the city, Yosef and Daud had learned the streets, gotten acclimated with the gang, and found work. Daud was a shoe shiner and Yosef an assistant at an auto mechanic shop.

Daud had spotted Yosef and Jogi approaching to pick him up for the film. His long hair, strands of which were covered in sweat, hid most of his forehead. He wiped the sweat and grime off his glistening face and into his blue pants. He gripped the shoeshine rag tighter in both hands and gave it a pop. A quick spit on the customer's already shiny black shoe, and his hands went to work, like the pistons of an engine, up and down, buffing the shoe.

Lahore was a unique city, which brought uncertain mornings, and unclear nights for Daud. In the beginning he followed Yosef wherever the older boy went. He did not tell Yosef about the recurrent dream he had about Akbar chasing him on the bus, and the nightmares eventually stopped. The congested traffic on McCleod Road scared him less with each passing day. Daud enjoyed it when Yosef took him for a bath at the canal after Daud finished working at a *gobar* (cow dung) drying factory before finding work as a shoe shiner. He ran away as fast as he could when the ball he struck hit a pedestrian on the street while playing cricket with other street urchins. On cold, smoky nights, he loved curling up in his shawl, sitting around the fire burning inside a small vat, eating peanuts with other boys and throwing shells into the flames. One morning he woke up and found a dog staring at him. It was a stray, black-and-white English springer spaniel with dried mud caked on him. The dog followed Daud all day, even when he was knee-deep at the *gobar* factory, sifting through wet cow dung.

"What is this?" Yosef arched his eyebrows as he saw Daud walking into Cafe Pyala with the dog. They named the dog Rambo.

Daud met Raja later in the summer that year on a hot afternoon. Daud was sitting along the banks of the canal, his legs dangling right above the water. Both banks of the canal, which ran in the middle of the road, were lined with weeping willows, eucalyptus, and numerous other trees. The murky water of the canal splashed each time someone jumped in—and there were hundreds of them, mostly young and teen-aged. Yosef sat right next to Daud, finishing the food he had bought from a street hawker.

"Could you imagine?" Yosef asked.

"Imagine what?"

"Jumping like this into Swat River, back home."

"No, never. The water is freezing in that river!" Daud shuddered.

"I bet it is nice and warm here."

"Looks that way."

"Then let's go!" Yosef got up.

"Go where?"

"For a dip, what else?"

"You're crazy!" Daud exclaimed.

"Follow me." Yosef ran toward the overpass, off of which everyone was jumping into the canal.

"I can't swim!" Daud cupped his mouth and yelled.

"Neither can I!"

And before Daud's eye, Yosef reached the overpass, shoved a couple of undecided children aside, and jumped. Splashing and frolicking, Yosef motioned Daud to follow suit. Daud shook his head. Then, after being called a wimp, a coward, and a chicken, Daud, grimacing, slowly walked up to the overpass. He could not believe that so many around him were jumping in and out of the canal so fiercely. They shrieked as they went airborne before landing in the water, and giggled as they climbed out of it, their clothes wet and dripping, only to do it all over again.

Daud carefully positioned himself on each brick being used as a step to get to the overpass and raised himself up. Looking down, he saw Yosef looking up, smiling. A small group of laughing children shoulder-butted Daud and jumped right into the water. Daud could tell they had just gotten got out of the canal by their wet clothes and running water streaks. Daud took another look down into the canal. His stomach churned. He had not jumped off anything higher than two feet. Gripping the railing and looking down, he was sure the overpass was much higher than his previous excursions. He cursed the moment when he had agreed to come down to the canal that day. Down below, Yosef had dipped and flipped one more time and now was motioning him to jump.

"Scared?" A voice came from behind Daud.

"I am— just— sorry—" Daud could not finish the sentence.

"Chicken!" Daud heard the voice say, and the next instant he felt a push. Then Daud was in the air, falling toward the water. Powerless to stop his descent, his eyes widened in disbelief while his arms and legs flapped in the air, his eyelids fluttered in the warm breeze, and his heart sank. He hit the water right next to Yosef. Panicked and ambivalent, Daud grabbed Yosef for support and gasped for air.

"Told you it will be fun!" Yosef splashed water on Daud's face.

The boy who pushed Daud had jumped right after him. He swam toward them.

"Did you like it?" he asked Daud, squeezing water off his hair with both hands.

"You!" Daud growled.

"Relax, puppy, your brother over there asked me to shove you down," the boy said.

Daud angrily turned to look at Yosef, who was laughing hysterically.

"You what?"

"You have to admit, it is a lot of fun," the boy said. "My name is Raja. What is yours?"

Daud went back up to the overpass with Raja few more times to jump into the water. By the end of the day, they were friends.

. . .

They were all looking for Yosef: Jogi, Raja, and Daud. Rambo followed Daud. On a crisp, cold December evening, they all walked the streets and asked others about Yosef's whereabouts. No one had seen him for days.

"Did he say anything to you?" Jogi asked Daud.

Daud remembered Yosef to be quiet lately. He seemed distracted, detached, absent-minded. He came out of deep thoughts when asked a question or urged to engage in a conversation. Upon being asked, he laughed it off and called Daud names.

"Maybe he got tired of your nagging and left," Raja teased.

Daud growled and punched Raja in the shoulder. Raja dodged the punch and provoked Daud to try again. They lost track of Jogi in the midst of their playfulness, who was talking to someone a few feet away.

"Let's go. I know where he is," Jogi said as Daud and Raja approached him.

They walked across the rail yard, alongside a red mosque, and through Lawrence Garden into a different neighborhood. Jogi stopped in front of a restaurant. His eyes searched through the glass windows before he spotted Yosef inside.

"You two wait here," Jogi said as he entered the room.

Daud and Raja put their hands around their eyes to make a canopy and peeked inside the window. Yosef was dressed in black pants and starched button-downed white shirt. His hair was neatly combed, and he seemed to have showered. Yosef was working as a waiter at this restaurant.

Jogi exchanged a few words with Yosef and walked out. Yosef followed shortly after. They stood at a distance. Daud and Raja could hear snippets. From the hand gestures, they could tell it wasn't a friendly conversation. They got closer.

"You must be crazy," they heard Jogi say.

. . .

Yosef had seen Neelam for the first time in October of that year. She was on her way to school, holding books in her hands, her head covered in a white *dupatta* (long headscarf). Yosef was on a motorcycle, riding it for a test run for a customer. He was stopped at a crossing when Neelam walked by with her friends, quipping, smiling. She wore a gray uniform with a white band around the waist. Her long, black hair glistened in the early morning sunlight floating through the misty fog. For a split second, Neelam's large gazelle-like eyes met Yosef's. Yosef stood at the same crossing every morning for the next few weeks, waiting for Neelam. It only took a few seconds for the girls to cross the road, and they'd be gone. Yosef waited every morning to see Neelam for those few seconds.

And they actually met when Yosef had gathered his courage and waited for her one afternoon outside the school. Neelam walked out of the school building with her friends and immediately noticed Yosef standing under a willow tree. Neelam's friends shrieked and giggled at the same time. Neelam, flushed, quickly adjusted the *dupatta* on her head, and started walking swiftly. They walked past Yosef, who dropped a rolled-up paper on the ground in front of them. Surya, one of Neelam's friends, saw the note. She quickly bent as if to scratch her ankle and picked up the note. Yosef saw them walking away. They quipped and laughed when Surya handed the note to Neelam. Before turning the corner, Neelam gave Yosef a long look.

The next day, Yosef waited for Neelam at Iqbal Park, adjacent to the school. According to the note he had dropped for Neelam, one he had written with the help of a boy who could write, by giving him dictation, they were to meet at three in the afternoon. Neelam arrived shortly before three, and then every day after that at the same time, to meet Yosef.

"You know you are playing with fire!" Jogi said after hearing that Neelam's father was a state employee and thus from a higher class than Yosef.

"I know what I am doing."

"And what is it exactly you are trying to do?"

Yosef thought of the fall afternoons when he waited for Neelam, the sound of leaves crushing under her feet announcing her arrival. The sound of her laughter, soft, like listening to the bells chime, stayed with him long after she was gone. And when she showed him the books she was studying, her fingers moving from line from line describing the images, he wished for time to stop.

"I am trying to be better."

"At the expense of abandoning those who care about you?"

Yosef thought of the rose he had given her the first time they met. Once dried, Neelam had put individual petals in her book as bookmarks. He recalled the smell of the lavender that infused the air when she was present.

Daud came closer and tugged on Yosef's pants. "Why haven't you been back to the Ring?" he asked.

"Don't waste your time, *bacha*. Some girl has cast her voodoo on him," Jogi laughed.

"I have to prove to Neelam that I am worthy."

"You are worthy of the streets!" Jogi shouted. "Abandoning your own for a *chokari* (girl)? What do you think will happen when her parents find out their daughter is going out with an urchin?"

"Maybe I don't want to be on the streets anymore," Yosef said.

"Is that why you have been avoiding us, avoiding the Ring?" Jogi cocked his head. "Embarrassed to be seen with us?"

"I will be back to see you soon, I promise." Yosef placed his hands on Daud's shoulder.

"You can take the venom out of a snake. But that won't stop it from biting. Just like that, you can wipe the grime off your face and put on pretty clothes. But that won't stop you from being a runaway, a street urchin." Jogi spat as he spoke, the saliva landing on Yosef's face.

Yosef kept his promise and visited Daud once or twice a week. He quit his job as an auto mechanic and started working full-time as a waiter. Upon Neelam's insistence, he started learning to read and write in Urdu. One early March afternoon, Yosef waited for Neelam at the park by the fountain. He placed the container next to him containing food from the restaurant he had packed for both of them, and took out a folded piece of paper. It was hand-written, by him. His fingers traced the characters of Urdu, a language derived from Persian and Arabic, that he'd turned into words, his first letter to Neelam, a stolen poem written by a famous poet:

Last night, your lost memories crept into my heart

as spring arrives secretly into a barren garden,

as a cool morning breeze blows slowly in a desert,

as a sick person feels well, for no reason.

He imagined the expression on her face when she'd read the poem. He neatly folded the paper back up and placed it in his pocket. Though still cold, there was a hint of spring in the air. Leaning over the fountain, he saw his reflection in the water. He closed his eyes and breathed in fresh air. Moments later, he heard the footsteps of someone approaching. "Neelam," he silently called out her name in his heart. Yosef opened his eyes and turned.

Neelam stood in front of him, covered by her *dupatta*. She was not wearing her school uniform. That was the first thing he noticed. The next thing that caught Yosef's attention was Neelam's hands. They were shaking. He followed her gaze. Her eyes were blood-shot, her face pale white. She had not slept all night, he could tell. Then he saw her lips quivering. With a puzzled look on his face, Yosef tried to make out what she was trying to say.

"Run," was all he could understand. And before he could react, a man appeared from behind a tree.

"Is that him?" the man asked. Without waiting for an answer, he ran toward Yosef. His punch hit Yosef's right jaw, throwing him into the fountain.

. . .

Jogi had just dealt the cards with three others at the table, when a boy stormed in through the doors of Café Pyala.

"*Dada*, come quick!" he yelled. "Hatim's got Yosef!"

The name itself was enough for everyone to scurry. Jogi asked if Hatim was coming in. Hatim was the name every street child was told to memorize, to steer clear of, and to avoid at any cost.

"You should come out, quick!" the boy motioned to Jogi.

Hatim stood outside the café, in front of the police jeep with its engine still running. He was a behemoth of a man, close to seven feet tall, with a girth to match his height and hands big enough to grab the necks of two children in each one.

"You know how I hate to come down to this slum, especially if it involves seeing you," he said as he saw Jogi walking out the café.

Hatim adjusted his beret and crushed a half-smoked cigarette under his boot. He had a thick, bushy moustache, an oily face with large pores, and large ears with dangling lobes. He opened the jeep door and dragged Yosef out by grabbing him by hair.

"One of yours?"

Jogi took one look at Yosef, and his heart sank. With swollen-shut purple eyes, black blood dried into his white shirt, and broken nose, Yosef had definitely been pummeled by Hatim's fists. He dangled in Hatim's hand like a puppet.

"Would you like to come inside and talk about it?" Jogi invited Hatim.

Hatim loosened his belt to allow his round stomach to overhang freely.

"I am not here to get a taste of your hospitality." Hatim dragged Yosef as he walked in a circle. "I just want to get the record straight."

Those who lived on the streets knew Hatim could come by anytime and knock over their fruit cart. He could pick up an urchin walking out of a brothel and beat him till he agreed to pay a portion of his daily wages to Hatim. There were stories about how he once picked up a street urchin involved in a street fight, drove him into forest miles away from Lahore, beat him, and left him there.

"This *harami*, living in the gutters, has the audacity to lure a girl from a noble family and meet her secretly," Hatim cleared his throat and announced.

"There must be a misunderstanding." Jogi wondered who had beaten Yosef the most, Hatim or the girl's father.

"There is no misunderstanding!" Hatim roared. "I tolerate you and your filth, so you will stay on your side. And to think that one of you can mingle with daughters of God-fearing people and stain their family honor! I am sure you can understand why I would want to bury him in front of your eyes." Hatim jerked Yosef's hair and tilted his face up.

Jogi wanted to remind Hatim of the hefty monthly fee he received every month to leave his gang alone. He chose to keep quiet.

"Is there anyone who can claim him?" Hatim asked the crowd.

Silence followed. They all hid behind counters, half-knocked-down walls, and balconies up above, watching from hidden corners as Yosef was tossed around by Hatim like a toy.

"Anyone?"

"This gang is all he has." Jogi chewed on each word as he spoke.

"A real *harami*, no mother, no father?" Hatim leaned over and whispered in Yosef's ear. His lips touched Yosef's ear lobe.

"You recognize your own type so well," Yosef said, and tried to open heavily bruised eyes. A drop of blood slid from one side of his mouth, down his chin. "I am impressed." A broken smile appeared on his face.

"Oh, no ... ." Jogi inhaled the cold wind through his mouth. The flesh in Hatim's arm shook as his fist, bigger than Yosef's face, slammed against it. Yosef's body, like a defeated boxer, tired and battered, plummeted to the ground. Jogi watched helplessly as, for the next several minutes,

Hatim pounced on Yosef's body, which had no sign of movement.

They all waited long after the dust settled behind Hatim's jeep before rushing to carry Yosef to the clinic.

"Why did Hatim not arrest Yosef?" someone at the waiting room asked.

"Because he wanted to make an example out of him," Jogi replied, sitting at the bench, his head resting against the wall. "And he did."

. . .

It was July now, a sunny mid-morning a few months later. Daud was negotiating the price and terms for a truck-loading job at the market square. The vast acres of park were crowded with tourists, panhandlers, and street children hustling to pick up labor for the day. The air was buzzing with loud voices and snippets from people talking in all directions.

"No, *sahib*, two hundred rupees, no less," Daud argued.

He had let go of his job as shoe shiner and started working at the market square, where there was more demand for physical labor, and more money. For the past four months he had earned a living for both Yosef and himself. He had rented a room, a small kitchen, and a bathroom with three other urchins and transferred Yosef there from the

Ring. Once a week, he ran to the Marie Adelaide Rehabilitation Center to get discounted medicine for Yosef.

The Marie Adelaide Rehabilitation tried to reach out to street children who needed shelter, food, tea, a shower, and rehabilitation from drugs and glue sniffing. A man named Constantine worked at the counter. He greeted visitors, offered assistance, and volunteered with the outreach program. He was a drug addict turned patient, volunteer, and now employee of the center. He had been admitted into rehab for inhaling a mixture of glue and paint. After completing rehabilitation, Constantine now provided services and guidance to other homeless children who fell into the trap of drug abuse.

Daud now walked over and sat down on the marble stairs that appeared to be the petals of the flower-like base of the minaret.

"Lost another one?" Yosef sat right next to him, his left arm still a little limp.

"It is the third since this morning," said Daud, frustrated. He had lost the bid for the truck-loading job. He felt tired.

"There will be others. Be patient."

Daud opened the world travel book given to him by Constantine. He had already gone through all the pictures three times. He imagined what words were written in the book about these places: perhaps directions on how to get there. Daud flipped to the page with a picture of African safari. The gold of the sun sprinkled on the vast wilderness of the Serengeti, where a lion taught its cub the art of hunting. Daud pictured himself standing there, watching the lion playfully pushing the restless cub to the side, while the cub grabbed and held on to his father's bowed tail. Daud wished he could be there to visit the foreign land. He wished he could fly.

A light breeze picked up and the pages fluttered.

"Eh, *bacha*, you're looking for work?"

Daud looked up and saw two teen-aged boys. One of them had a scar running down his left cheek and a mole under his nose. The other seemed taller and had a moustache.

"Our master there needs help. You will need to come with us to his house."

Daud gazed past the two teenagers and saw a man standing at a distance, with dark glasses and neatly pressed clothes. Daud nodded in agreement.

6 THE LETTER

October 15, 1999

The red brick, single-story building stood in the city's busy court district. The front was secured with a large wrought-iron gate. An arched black plaque was affixed to each end of the gate and announced, in bold, shimmering gold letters, "Lahore Police Station, Kantt branch."

The gates opened to a courtyard with a cobblestone walkway in the middle, stretched out in the shape of a T. Both sides along the walls were covered with trimmed shrubs, and seasonal flowers, swinging in the light, cool breeze. The building across the courtyard was painted pale yellow, with dark green windows frames. The midday sun shone directly above the building, giving it a shimmering gold look.

The room inside was large, and open on both ends. The back wall was split in the middle, and a narrow, dark hallway led toward the back of the building, with a couple more rooms on each side. The front room looked just like an office from the

British-era '30s and '40s. There were two desks on each side of the walls, each with throngs of files and furnished with an old-fashioned, black rotary phone. Tall metal file cabinets were placed against the walls by the main door. There was an old wooden console table on the east side of the room, with a black tabletop fan running full speed. Occasionally its turning blades perturbed a loose paper, making it flutter.

Sunshine filtered through the window panes like spotlights, illuminating dust particles in the air. One drifting gleam landed right on the yellow manila envelope that lay on the table, its contents half exposed. The superintendent, a tall, wheat-complexioned man with a bearded long face, sat in the chair behind the table and stared at the envelope as if a ghost was about to jump out and grab his neck. Except for the buzzing white noise of fan blades running at on high, there was no other sound around him.

A few hours ago he had thought someone had played a sick joke on him, and he'd tossed the letter and envelope into the wastebasket. "Sick bastards," he muttered under his breath, and blamed the media and western movies for corrupting young minds. But his last two visitors had compelled him to take another look at the package and go through the letter one more time, more thoroughly this time. He wiped the sweat from the back of his neck and leaned over to read again:

Confession

"My name is Javed Iqbal, and this is my confession. I have killed one hundred children. I drugged all of my victims before killing them and dissolved their corpses in sulfuric and hydrochloric acid. All the details of the murders are noted in the diary and the thirty-two-page notebook that has been placed in the room and has also been sent to the law enforcement authorities.

"I could have killed five hundred if I wanted to; that would not have been a problem. But the pledge I had taken was of one hundred children. I respected my pledge.

"I hate this world. I am not ashamed of my actions, and I am ready to die. I have no regrets. I killed one hundred children. My mother cried for me after what this society did to me. I want one hundred mothers to cry for their children. My actions will make my victims' mothers weep. I have sent their sons to the next world without coffins, through the gutter.

"I invite you to come and take a look for yourself. Once you discover what I have achieved, it will shock the world. No one but God could have stopped me. But where was God when I had my way with these children and killed 1, 2, 3, 10, 15, 25, 50, 100 of them? I have no fear of death nor of the judgment of this world or hereafter. My mission is accomplished. They got what they deserved. This society got what it deserved. I have lived through the pain inflicted on me by this world. Now it is time for this society to lick its wounds and explain to this world what happened to one hundred boys, sacrificed to my rage.

"Why one hundred, your inquisitive mind wonders? I want you to feel the pain I went through, one hundred times more. My actions will send a message to this world and to the families of those children about what it feels like when you lose someone. To take a piece of your heart away from you, is the greatest feeling in the world.

"I will lead you to it; guide you to the signs to follow to this place where one hundred young souls took their last breath. If you listen closely, you will hear the screams in the air, pleading for mercy, begging for their life to be spared. But it's all quiet now. It's calm. They are all gone. I may end my life by jumping into the river. But then again, what would be the point of accomplishing my goal if I don't get to enjoy it? Come, come to witness that what I say is true."

"167 Ravi Road."

. . .

Earlier the same day

Saif dashed through the parked motor cycles leaning on sidewalk stalls, panting and wiping off a constant stream of sweat before it got into his eyes. Pedestrians on the footway turned back and cursed at him for shouldering them aside. Oblivious, Saif did not hear a single word. His mind was engrossed with the image of the room in the dim light and the conversation with the neighbor. The image of his brother's clothes lying on the pile ran over and over in his mind. Was it possible that he might have been mistaken, he questioned himself. Could those have been someone else's clothes?

What about the bracelet? He could never have mistaken the bracelet, no, not that. Any remaining doubts of being wrong about the clothes vanished as the assurance of recognizing the bracelet sank in.

He had stayed up all night. Fatigued and drained of energy, his brain had been telling his body to shut down. Sleep was miles away from him, a figment of imagination like a fairy tale. He hobbled faster, cut corners, and dodged oncoming traffic as he hurried to his destination.

The door slammed open, which startled Mina. She ran to the door and saw Saif. He stood there for few moments in silence, desperately trying to catch his breath.

"We have to go, *amma*," he finally uttered through his parched throat.

Minutes later, they were rushing toward the police station.

"Tell me once again what you saw," Mina said loudly while maintaining her speed. She did not ask why Saif had not been back to see her. Many times she had thought she would greet Saif with a slap on his face when she saw him. She thought of grabbing him by the ear for not returning any messages she had left for him. But the face of her son, drained of color, made her forget the anguish she had been through for the past two months. Saif stopped and waited for her, struggling to walk with her face half covered, to catch up before repeating the story of his visit to the house and meeting the neighbor.

"Say something," Saif said after he finished. Mina kept her head down and walked. They came to a stop light and waited for the signal to turn green. "Say that I lost your son." Saif's voice quivered when he spoke. "Say that you trusted me to keep Raja safe, and I failed."

"Walk faster," was all Mina said in reply. She wiped her eyes with her *dupatta*, adjusted it back on her head, and continued to walk swiftly.

She was frantically fighting a battle of heart and mind. Her heart continued to give her hope, scenarios that might have led to a different outcome and would mean the safety of her missing son. Saif did not see Raja in the room, she argued with herself. What about the clothes? Raja easily could have been given different clothes for the job.

"Finding Raja's clothes and bracelet does not mean anything," she said out loud.

Yet in the back of her mind, a voice kept telling Mina something had gone terribly wrong. So many nights she woke up from sleep, jolted and soaked in sweat. The nightmares kept crawling back, vanishing as she sprang right up in bed. But she knew it had something to do with her son, Raja.

Saif felt nervous going to the police with his mother. He was one of the urchins who had hidden behind a storefront and watched Hatim taking pleasure in beating Yosef like a rag doll. He was well aware of the stories that hit the airwaves on the streets, of the recklessness and brutality of the police. Living on the street, he had learned that they were better off enduring the injustice done to them than to go to the police for help. He recalled Jogi and his warnings. But this was one iniquity he could not ignore and live with. He looked at Mina sprinting in front of him. She needs to know, he thought, we all need to know what happened to Raja. He offered a silent prayer and continued to walk toward the police station.

They both entered the black gate and walked the cobblestone walkway into the police station. A constable sitting at a table looked up and gazed at the boy and woman standing in front of him, breathing heavily. He then looked down at his watch. The smell of body odor and sweat wafting from Saif and Mina entered his nostrils. His eyebrows arched as he squinted at them.

"*Salam.*" Saif raised his right arm and touched his forehead with the back of his hand. "We are here to file an FIR (first information report)," Saif said to the constable, a tall, thin man with a pencil moustache on his face.

Mina stood there, her face covered below the nose by her *dupatta*. The corner of her *kameez* fluttered in the air.

"Who is the woman?" the constable asked and did not offer them to sit down.

Mina felt the constable's gaze penetrating deep into her. She recognized the look, even after fifteen years, from the night when so many eyes had crawled over her body. The night when she had wished the sun would not rise the next day and that she would drown in the darkness of her own sorrow. She wrapped the *dupatta* tightly around her.

"What's the offence?" the constable asked after learning Mina was Saif's mother.

"We are not sure," Saif replied.

The constable frowned and sank further into the chair.

"You want me to file a complaint for a crime that may or may not have occurred?"

"My younger son has been missing," Mina spoke. "He vanished two months ago."

The constable shifted his gaze to her, an intent stare, as if contemplating how to respond to her.

"Let's hope the mother has a bit more brain than the son," he finally said. "Tell me all about it."

Mina stared at the pencil that the constable rotated in his hand while listening to the story. Occasionally, he'd glance at Mina.

"Where do you and your brother live?" the constable asked Saif.

"We ... *sahib* ... we ...," Saif fumbled.

"A house, room, maybe a hut?"

"We left the house and now live on our own," Saif answered.

"You and your brother are street urchins, runaways?"

Saif stood there and did not say anything in response.

"How do you know he didn't spend the money he made that day on drugs?"

The constable leaned back in the chair and swiveled it. Silence followed. He stared at both Saif and Mina. His attention then shifted to Mina's hands. They were shaking.

"Through this door I see many street urchins come and go." He continued to swivel as he spoke. "They are dragged in for stealing, taking drugs, prostitution, panhandling, gang fights ... and the list goes on and on, my unwelcome guests." He waved his hands toward Saif and Mina. "I am trying really hard not to get upset over you attempting to ruin my morning."

"My brother is not a druggie." Saif's voice tensed. He moved forward and held the back of the chair in front of him.

"A runaway, thrown out of home, street urchin—sure!" the constable taunted. "For all I know he is hiding in a dark alley somewhere behind a dumpster getting high on glue."

"That is not true. I know Raja," Saif protested.

"Are you calling me a liar, boy?" the constable slammed his fist on the table, startling Saif and Mina. His hand reached for his baton. The image of Yosef lying on the street and being pounded by Hatim ran through Saif's mind. He grabbed Mina's hand and took a step back.

"There are others, too, who have disappeared, just like my brother," Saif said in a shaken voice, gulping down his saliva.

"This is a city of millions of people," the constable snickered. "People disappear here by the minute. You're keeping track of who comes and goes?"

"No."

"Then what, *bacha*? Tell me."

"His clothes, in the house. The bracelet—"

"And the thought never entered your tiny brain that he might have voluntarily changed into different clothes, before hopping onto the bus and leaving for another city, far away from here?" The constable was now on the other side of the table, the side where Saif and Mina were standing.

Regrets poured into Saif's heart. This was a bad idea, he thought.

"We don't know how else to find my brother." He felt defeated, helpless.

The superintendent walked into the room, holding a letter.

"What is this commotion all about?" he demanded. The constable explained the situation to his superior.

"Do you think we have no better things to do then to waste our time on runaways?" the superintendent said. With his back to them, he walked up to a file cabinet and started sifting through drawers.

"We came here looking for help," Mina spoke, her voice broken and trembling.

The superintendent turned to look at her. A shadow of recognition ran across his face as he slowly walked up to her.

"Is your name Mina?" he asked.

Mina kept staring at the wall in front of her. Her heart pounded uncontrollably. She felt Saif's hand clutching hers tightly.

The superintendent circled around her and gave her an intent look.

"From Rampura?"

No one had connected her to that town for over a decade. Rampura, her hometown, was buried deep in her past. How could a stranger know her and the village she was born in?

"You are Khadim Ali's daughter, aren't you?" The superintendent cocked his head and looked her straight in the eyes.

She had not seen *baba* or *amma* since the day she had left Rampura. That was the condition, she was told, if they were to ever restore the family name and honor: they were never to see Mina again. She was as good as dead to them. Who was this man, digging into the grave of her past, exposing the rotten corpses in front of Saif?

"Have a seat." The superintendent pulled out a chair. "You too, son," he offered Saif.

The confused look on constable's face deepened when the superintendent asked him to fetch water for mother and son.

"My name is Yunus," the superintendent introduced himself to Mina. "I am from Rampura, also."

Mina's terrified gaze slowly shifted toward the superintendent. Within the beard, wheat complexion, and long chin she searched for a hint that might lead to forgotten memories. There was nothing.

"You …" her lips quivered.

"I lived across the field from where you lived." The superintendent understood the question. "My sincere apologies for addressing you like this." Mina could not recall the last time she had heard a tone as soft as that.

"You have no reason to know of me, or recognize me." He handed her a glass of water. "But I remember you. As a kid, I used to watch you take evening tea to your father. I remember the mole on your left cheek."

Mina's head spun. There had been a boy in the village who watched her, day after day, walking down the unpaved road, frolicking, jumping, picking berries fallen from the trees. What a cruel joke this was that time had played on her.

"You have two sons now?" he was asking.

That boy remembered little Mina, she thought. How intense must have been the gaze that made him remember that girl, even after all those years, when she was a ruin.

"I remember the day you left Rampura for Lahore," Yunus said.

He had been there; he had seen her. Mina imagined a little boy enshrouded behind a tree, watching her. He had seen, as she walked like the undead, stained and dishonored, saying goodbyes, vowing not to return.

"I am very sorry for what happened to you." Yunus's head was down when he spoke.

And Mina melted, her entire being liquefied. To know there was someone out there who knew she did not deserve what had happened to her was a feeling she was not prepared for. Mina covered her face and wept.

. . .

Now, after Saif and Mina had left, Yunus sat and stared at the manila envelope one more time. The letter that had arrived in it sat in front of him. He had assured Mina he would look into Raja's disappearance. He told her it was possible Raja had gotten tired of his current situation and gotten on the bus to another city. He now wondered if Saif and Mina were actually telling the truth and needed help. He jolted as his chain of thought was broken by the sound of a phone ringing. The chief commissioner was on the other line.

"I am holding a letter in my hand sent to me this morning," the voice on the other end said. "It reads, 'My name is Javed Iqbal, and this is my confession. I have killed one hundred children.'" The commissioner read on. Yunus kept listening, his eyes staring at the letter in his hand. The commissioner was reading him the same letter. Multiple copies of this letter had been sent to several stations.

"Do you know anything about this?" the commissioner finished the letter and asked.

"Can't say that I do, sir. A similar letter has been sent to me as well." Once again Yunus thought of Mina.

"Please have it checked out for authenticity."

"What is your inclination, sir?" Yunus asked.

"It seems like part of some crazy hoax to me," the commissioner answered. "Unless there are an unusually large number of missing person reports filed, I don't think it is legit." He then asked, "Has there been an unusual number of reports?"

"No sir, not to my knowledge." Yunus ran his hand over his cheekbones. He felt the stubbled shadow creeping up sooner than usual. He contemplated whether he should mention Mina.

"That is strange."

"Yes, sir."

"Check with other stations and check for recent reports of missing children, abduction, kidnapping, and such."

"Yes, sir."

"We don't want to take any chances even if it is a hoax, and even if it says the only children involved are street urchins."

"I will get right on it, sir," Yunus obediently replied, and hung up. He sprang off his chair and ran to the back room.

"Show me the missing FIR reports for the past two months," he exclaimed to the constable there, who had just lit a cigarette and was in the middle of letting exhaled smoke spiral up in the air. The constable rummaged through stacks of ledger books and dragged one out. The settled dust on the rectangular book scattered in the air.

"How many?"

"Sir?"

"How many came in like the last one?"

The constable ran his fingers through the pages and replied, "Ten."

"Call other branches across the city and find out how many reports they have of missing children." Yunus frantically flipped through the pages.

"Do you mind telling me, sir, what is the matter?" The constable shifted in his chair impatiently. This sounded like a lot more work than he was used to.

"This might not be a hoax," Yunus waved the letter in the constable's face.

"No hoax?"

"The chief commissioner has received the same letter. I have orders from above to check it all out."

The constable grabbed the letter and read it.

"I can assure you, sir, that we would have been the first ones to know if there were any such crimes going on," the constable announced in a calm and confident tone.

"Pick up the phone and get busy. Let your wife know that you will not be coming home any time soon." Yunus turned to go back to his room and saw another constable lurching in, holding a piece of paper.

"Don't tell me!" Yunus looked at him and then nodded at the paper he was holding.

"Sir, we need to hurry." The constable barely caught his breath.

"Hurry for what? What are you taking about?

"The newspaper agencies received this letter, and they are on their way to this address."

Superintendent Yunus looked at the letter. It was the same letter sent to him and the chief commissioner, and the address was:

167 Ravi Road.

. . .

Dust clouds gathered as the minivan sped through the streets. Winter was coming, short days had brought diminutive shadows, and there was a slight chill in the air. There were three passengers in the vehicle. An expensive camera lay in the lap of one of them. The back of the vehicle was cluttered with loose paper, empty food wraps, a tripod, and a microphone. Both sides of the minivan were painted with the insignia "National Morning

Star," which was one of the leading newspapers in the city. The driver had clear instructions to use his driving skills to navigate through the narrow, overly congested streets of Old Lahore. He made his way through by constant honking, cutting off other cars, veering around terrified pedestrians, and splashing through pools of muddy rainwater. Annoyed passersby showed hand gestures and yelled at the reckless driver of the minivan. The echoes of their wails slammed against the closed windows of the vehicle and shattered in the air. The heedless passengers of the minivan were unaware of the chaotic mess and curses they were leaving behind.

"How long before we get there?" one of the men yelled at the driver from the backseat.

"Give or take, ten more minutes," the driver responded without turning his head. He cursed at the auto rickshaw in front of him blocking the intersection.

"I still don't believe this." The man with the bouncing camera on his lap nodded at the letter in his fellow passenger's hands. His name was Asghar. He appeared to be in his mid-thirties, bald at the top, with droopy, bloodshot eyes behind round-framed glasses. The engine of the van sounded weak. It made loud sputtering noises, making it difficult to converse even with all the windows closed. There was also a deep, constant humming sound inside the cabin coming from underneath the minivan's floor.

"If it is some type of joke, I am not ready for it," his companion replied. He had a full head of salt-and-pepper hair with a matching goatee. His name was Salman. "But we have to go where there might be a lead."

"I won't be surprised if the address of the location turns out to be a vacant lot." Asghar laughed. "But what if there is a slight bit of truth to it?" His laughter vanished quickly with the question.

"Then, my friend, we have got a front page story for tomorrow's print," Salman replied. Resting his head on the headrest, he took a peek out the window. They were getting on the Ravi River bridge.

"But, I mean, who writes something like this? It couldn't possibly be true!" Asghar took the letter from Salman's hands and waved it in the air.

"To answer your question, either someone with a twisted brain and lots of time, or …"

"Or?"

"Or an actual killer." Salman rubbed his goatee, smirked, and winked at Asghar. His words hovered in the still air as the van hit a speed bump and bounced in the air.

"Yow!" Salman exclaimed to the driver when his head hit the roof. "Get us there before any other, up-to-no-good news agency gets wind of it. I want this story to be all mine, if there is one." The driver shrugged his shoulders.

The van took the turn into Ravi Road, half a block from the 167 address in the letter. An unmarked conversion van was already parked in front of the house.

"Fuck!" Salman exclaimed, irritated.

"How did they find out?" Asghar murmured.

"Looks like we are not exclusively the privileged ones who received the letter." Salman grunted and opened the van's sliding door, which had come to a crawl.

The driver pulled the van up a few feet behind the conversion van and both newspapermen got out. There were two other men standing in front of the house.

"I don't believe this!" one of them said, as he saw Asghar and Salman approaching. All four men huddled in front of the house and exchanged nods and looks.

"I assume it makes no sense for me to ask what you two might be doing here." Salman let out a chuckle as he spoke.

"I still think this is a prank. No one in his right mind would commit a crime and then publicize it." A short, pudgy man with a thick moustache and glistening hair emerged from a dark corner. He quickly put on his sunglasses as bright sunlight made his eyes squint. "I am telling you. This is a cheap stunt to gain a few minutes of fame. That's all."

"My friend over here shares the same sentiment." Salman pointed at Asghar.

"If you are so convinced this is a prank, then why are you here?" the man with sunglasses taunted.

"Let's not go there," Salman smiled. "We all know why we are here."

"Prank or not, we are here to find out. Let's do it."

"The question is, how do we get in? This place looks deserted."

"I wouldn't mind climbing over."

"Sure. Don't mind the neighbors or broad daylight," Salman snickered.

"You got any better ideas?"

"Not really. I am starting to regret the decision to come here in the first place."

The man with sunglasses nodded at his companion, who vanished behind the conversion van for a while. He returned with a bolt cutter in his hand. The man wearing sunglasses looked at Salman and Asghar and said, "We cut the padlock."

He grabbed the handles of the cutter in both hands and chopped it in the air. "If the police get in this house before us, everything will be sealed and tampered with, and we won't know if it is true or not."

They all nodded in agreement. The man who fetched the cutter proceeded toward the iron gate. Two doors down, a young boy poked his head out the front door of his house. He saw four men standing in front of the abandoned house. He vanished behind closed doors as quickly as he had appeared.

After a few struggled attempts, the padlock slammed against the gate and broke. Rusted hinges screeched as the men pried the gate open. A tall lasora-gum berry tree stood in the middle of the veranda. Wild grass and weeds surrounded the trunk. No one had cared for the tree for quite some time. They entered into the open veranda, which had a cobblestone floor, exposed shoulder-high brick walls, and a stressed tree in the middle.

Dried leaves crunched under their feet when they walked. Asghar turned on the camera and set the flash, ready to go.

"Wait. We have to be sure of what we are looking for," Salman said.

Beyond the veranda, behind the tree, was a closed door, which according to the letter opened into a room. All four men gingerly approached the door, their senses alert for any sign of movement. An eerie silence followed until a whiff of cool breeze passed through, dragging dried leaves on the floor that made a ruffling noise.

"Friends, the moment of truth has arrived," Salman said to the rest hoarsely, and pushed the door open. The old, chipped wood made a crackling noise and gave way to darkness inside. A burst of stale, rotting air escaped the room and slammed across their faces. The men squinted. With one hand covering his nose, Salman ran his fingers blindly on the wall to the right of the door, feeling for a switch.

"Here, I found it," Asghar said from behind him, and flicked the switch he had discovered on the left wall. Pale yellow light slowly flooded the room, chasing off the darkness, meagerly reaching the room's far corners.

Their eyes slowly adjusted to the room, taking in what lay all around: a mostly empty room with a wicker bed, a chair, and a side table. A heart-sinking feeling came as their eyes rested on the vats placed in the far left corner. Two long bones lay on top of one of them. The other had a notebook on top. The breeze coming in from the door fluttered its pages. None of them moved. It felt cold and eternally silent, as if they have been shoved underwater. Until one of them let out a choked squeak.

"Oh, my God!" he said.

Wide eyed, they all turned to follow his gaze toward the right wall. The wall, almost all of it, was covered with pictures. They were pictures of teenage boys, some smiling, others with a confused look on their faces as they stared at the camera. Asghar dropped the letter from his hands, and it glided its way down to the floor. Deprived of sufficient light, they stepped forward to take a closer look.

"One hundred," the man holding the bolt cutter muttered.

"What?"

"There are one hundred pictures on this wall."

"Just like what the letter said." Asghar ran his hand over his chin.

"What did the letter say?"

"'I have assaulted and killed one hundred children.'"

"I'll be damned," Salman said. "Turn on the camera and start shooting." His lips moved, his words sounding as if he were coming out of a deep sleep, as he addressed Asghar without shifting his gaze from the wall.

"It may not be a hoax after all."

"This is nothing like any of us have ever seen before."

A bright flash of the camera splashed on the wall, illuminating the pictures, filling the room with bright light.

"Take a look at this," the man with sunglasses shouted. All eyes turned to the left. There on the floor lay a pile of clothes and shoes of different sizes, permeating the room with the smell of mold and rotten laundry.

Reality slowly seeped into their minds. The letter was not sent from a bored teenager who had watched one too many western movies. A crime had been committed in that house. The room howled with the voiceless cries of its victims.

"I don't believe this." Asghar grabbed his head with both hands and paced back and forth. "Unbelievable."

Salman hurried up to the vats and grabbed the notebook. "It's only a matter of seconds before the police get here," he said, as he saw the other reporter approaching.

"Stop wherever you are!" a loud husky voice boomed from the door, startling the men inside the room. "Do not touch anything. This is the police," Yunus said as he entered the room.

Outside the house, the little kid from two houses down had gathered his parents and a few other neighbors. After calling the police, they stood outside and gossiped about what those men might be doing inside the abandoned house in their neighborhood.

. . .

At the far end of the porch by the police station lay the clothes and shoes recovered from 167 Ravi Road, the crime scene. An old man crouched at the edge of the pile and rummaged through it. His days-old beard had more shades of white then black. There seemed to be a plea in his eyes, hoping not to find what he was looking for. One could tell that he wanted to hang on to the very last thread of hope that his son might still be alive. And that hope would be sustained if his son's belongings were not in the pile of clothes he so feverishly shuffled. His hands crawled to a halt, his eyes stony at the sight of the pair of shoes his son wore. Running his fingers along the stitches on the shoe, his eyes welled and he started sobbing. All hope was gone.

Superintendent Yunus and the constables were cooped up in a room inside the station, doors shut. The front porch outside the room was mobbed with people, some struck with grief and others standing quietly, their mouths covered with their hands, stunned by the news. Some in the crowd sifted through the wrecked clothes and tried to find an article that would jog a memory. Among them, a woman let out a scream as she spotted the yellow shirt her son had worn the day he disappeared. Clutching what possibly was the last remnants of her offspring, she let out another scream and slapped her chest with bare hands. Others rushed to hold and console her before she plummeted to the floor.

It was not an everyday occurrence at the police station. No one was prepared for it. The setting sun had disappeared behind a stray patch of cloud, making autumn feel much colder. For many at the police station, this part of the day meant time to call it a day and go home. But it was not the case today.

There were many others just like the chest-beating woman and bereaved old man, mourning and tearing through the pile of clothes to identify their loved one's belongings. The screaming was deafening and heart-shattering to the crowd gathered outside the station. Inside the room, the superintendent held his head between his hands. The sound of lament outside pierced inside with all its fury, despite the closed shutters and locked doors. The black rotary-dial phone rang constantly, and after answering it for the ninth time one of the constables slammed it on the table.

'This is ridiculous," he grunted.

"Sounds impossible," another joined in.

"How are we going to handle this?" The first constable glared at the superintendent sitting across the table. Superintendent Yunus slowly poked his head out of the cave of his hands and stared back.

"You are asking me, you imbeciles?" he bellowed. "The situation could have been contained had you reached the crime scene before those journalists."

He wondered if Mina was outside in the crowd, shifting through the clothes to locate her son's belongings. He wished he could open the door and let her in. He wished he could tell her he had been inside the room where Raja might have taken his last breath. The constable was responding: "Sir, we arrived at the scene as fast as we could. But they were already there, tampering with evidence and filming the scene."

"They acted on the same tip we had. It was just a timing issue, who got to the finish line of the race first." A fellow constable came to his colleague's defense.

The letter from the killer had been sent to several news agencies and law enforcement authorities. Someone outside slammed their hand on an outside window pane. The sound of it startled everyone inside the station.

"Don't give me excuses." Yunus sounded frustrated. "We should have secured the house before anyone reached it."

At that moment, yet another constable emerged from a back room.

"You may want to put the phone back on." He nodded at the phone receiver dangling off the cradle. "The commissioner is trying to reach you, sir," he addressed Yunus.

Feeling closed in by the anxious and resentful eyes around him, the constable replaced the receiver. The phone rang instantly. Heavy hearted, the superintendent picked it up.

"Sir, yes sir," he spoke to the voice on the line. With his head down, he rested his elbows on his knees as he spoke. "I am afraid so, sir. All evidence suggests that a crime has been committed … I am sorry, sir, I ... No, we have not discovered any bodies yet ... Except for... Sir, yes sir ... Except that our men recovered what appears to be human bones sitting on top of one of the vats found in the room."

Silence followed for the next few seconds. Yunus pressed the phone against his ear and listened intently. The constables could hear the commissioner's forceful and demanding voice transmitting over the phone's handset.

"Yes sir, except for the clothes and shoes that apparently belonged to the victims." Yunus found it difficult to describe. "That is being sorted by family members for identification. They had already arrived at the crime scene, sir. News agencies across town received the same letter," Yunus was explaining.

The superintendent could feel the tiny drops of water accumulating on his forehead. He loosened the collar of his shirt. He clutched the phone tighter. The crowd outside was getting louder and louder. A few banged on the door and demanded explanations.

"I am not really sure, sir. I can use a little advice, though," Yunus spoke.

What followed were some grunting sounds on the other end.

He listened for several minutes in silence with occasional nods before hanging up. Yunus felt his head spinning, and his face was flushed.

"We need to dispatch news bulletins to all stations around the city," he addressed the apprehensive constables circling him. "See if any family members remember with whom the missing children were last seen. Go back to the crime scene and interview neighbors. Find out who came in and out of that house. Have the evidence scanned for any fingerprints. That should give you enough to start with, don't you think?" The superintendent's voice echoed in the room despite the commotion outside.

"Get right on it. And try not to mess too many things up."

The superintendent sank deeply into his chair after all the constables had left. His eyes stared at the glass of the closed window, the shutters showing the dark silhouettes outside the room, pacing, circling, slamming against the walls. What was he supposed to tell them about what had happened to their lost children? How was he to find an alleged murderer of one hundred children who exposed his own crime by inviting the world over?

. . .

The news spread like a conflagration throughout the city within twenty-four hours. Live news feeds were sent from one news agency to the next. The residents of Lahore woke up to digest this front page headline:

ONE HUNDRED CHILDREN KIDNAPPED, ASSAULTED, AND KILLED.

Many wondered if there was a publishing error from last night's run at the printing press. Nonetheless, newspapers sold within hours, and by midday there wasn't a single copy to be found. People turned to radio and TV. Newscasters announced the new discovery, crime experts offered their opinions, and reporters provided details live outside the house where the crime had taken place.

"What you see behind me is a house where an alleged serial killer made a shrine of the young victims he murdered," one reporter stared at the camera and uttered into his microphone. "Our sources tell us that the murder suspect took pictures of his victims and pinned them on the wall before committing the crime."

Another reporter cleared his throat few feet away.

Yet another tapped his earpiece and said, "Wait, I am getting word that a letter of confession was sent to the police."

The phones rang constantly at the police stations, hospitals, and news agencies. Cafés, restaurants, barber shops, and any other venues with access to TV or radio were packed. All eyes and ears were mesmerized by what they saw and heard. The city had witnessed one of the worst crimes committed in its history. One angry spokesperson from a social not-for-profit organization came on TV, slammed his fist on a table, and demanded, "Why is it that one hundred children disappeared before our very eyes and hardly any missing reports were filed with the police and no eyebrows raised?"

His speech and those of many others like him were the focal point of discussion on thousands of television screens across the country, including the large electronics showroom on Mall Road. The storefront's large glass window showcased several TVs aligned on top of each other in a brick-wall pattern. Among the audience on the sidewalk watching the grainy screens was Yosef, staring at the images on the TVs.

. . .

The vista wasn't any different at Café Pyala that evening. The air was saturated with loud noises. All one could hear was snippets. It was a standing-room-only crowd, a patronage the owner had not seen since the cold winter blast several years ago. An old black-and-white television sat on top of a cart. It had old-style shiny knobs to change the channels and fine tune; its rabbit-ear antenna was wrapped in aluminum foil for better reception.

All eyes were fixed on the screen. The grainy images of a news broadcast danced on the screen in vertical waves. The reception was bad. Occasionally the image became distorted due to the passing of a plane or interference with another frequency. A boy from the crowd, sitting close to the television, would get up and give it a big thump on the side each time the vision distorted. It worked.

They all watched with intense faces and heavy breath. There were video clips of people gathered outside the police station, grieving, mourning, and going through the remains of clothes found. Then the police commissioner came on. He promised to use all possible resources and capture the culprit. His answer to the majority of the questions was, "I am not sure, but it is under investigation." The scene changed, and a camera showed the house where the crime took place, starting at the top level and working its way down before halting in front of the news reporter's face. The reporter recounted the details of the story. The broadcast was a repeat, and many had seen the footage before.

The mood turned dismal as pictures of some of the identified victims came on. Several in the crowd recognized one or two faces on TV and gasped in anguish. Saif walked in with Yosef and looked around. They spotted Jogi sitting at the far end and waved. A few minutes passed by in silence after they took seats next to him.

"You did a brave thing going to the police," Jogi said to Saif.

"There was no other choice."

"You could have come to me."

"I did come to you," Saif snapped. "But after seeing what I saw inside the house, your advice for solace and patience was not enough."

Saif thought about the constable tightening his grip around the baton at the police station. And the conversation superintendent had with *amma.* He had not been to see her after their visit to the police station. There wasn't time or energy to talk about anything else other than the urchins gone missing, including Raja.

"They would have found the house, even if you hadn't." Yosef took a cigarette out of the pack sitting on the table.

"What do you mean?"

"That *harami* sent letters to the police and newspapers, telling them to come to the house where he … ." He stopped talking. Saif and Jogi looked at him.

"I am responsible for his death," Yosef continued.

His wounds had healed. For months after the beating, he had lain on the mattress, covered in bandages, unable to move, waiting every day for Daud to come back. In his mind, Daud had brought him back to life. It was Daud who had transferred him to a room from the Ring, earned a living for two, dashed out to the pharmacy on nights when Yosef's body baked in high fever. Yosef listened, crippled by his wounds, when Daud lay next to him each night and told Yosef he would take care of him. He reminded Yosef how he had rescued them from the carpet factory. Unable to respond, Yosef heard Daud say how grateful he was for what Yosef did for him. Daud did not understand why Yosef had left him and the rest of the gang for Neelam, a girl. But he did not ask.

"I brought Daud here. I am responsible for what happened to him." Yosef clutched Daud's shirt, which he had collected from the clothing pile at the police station.

"No one knew." Jogi placed his hand on Yosef's shoulder. "No one could predict what was taking place right in our backyard."

"Don't be ridiculous. You helped him escape from the hell of slavery," Saif said.

"Only to shove him into the hands of a serial killer."

"Don't own a guilt that does not belong to you," Jogi said.

"This is my hell. I belong in it," Yosef said coarsely. "I brought Daud to this city, and it swallowed him." He punched the table.

"Give it time, *bacha*. Let time heal your pain."

"This lousy shirt is all that is left of him," Yosef cried.

"Shhhh." Jogi rubbed his hand on Yosef's shoulder. "It will get better. It always does."

"There is only one way I will be able to sleep at night now," Yosef said in a hoarse voice. "There is only one way I will ever find closure."

Yosef raised his head and stared at Jogi and Saif through his bloodshot eyes.

"I must find him." There was an icy coldness in his voice. "I must find Javed before anyone else does."

7 CONSTANTINE

November 4, 1999

It was the usual traffic chaos like any other day on Ichra Road, one of the most congested and busy roads in the city, which cut right through the main business district. Traffic constables in white uniforms were at all major intersections, perched on top of the elevated pedestals in the middle of the roads. They blew whistles with the most breath that could be mustered by their lungs, trying to control the traffic. The shrill whistling sound was lost to the din of honking cars, loud auto rickshaws, and noisy buses emitting black smoke. Some of the constables had to risk their lives by stepping in the middle of oncoming traffic, motioning the oncoming traffic to stop, which otherwise had no intention of halting at the red light.

A taxi driver cursed and yelled at the motorcycle rider who cut him off, leaving the taxi stuck behind a horse carriage. A few rows behind, a rickshaw didn't bother to wait for the red light to change, decided to make the left turn anyway by pulling into the opposite lane, and almost hit a pedestrian. The air was filled with smog, the constant sound of horns honking, and the ear-shattering sound of whistles.

Away from all that mayhem, on one of the nearby side streets, a van pulled up in front of an old building set amid more modern architecture. It was a two-story structure, long and narrow. The front façade was painted in yellow and white. Two men sat in the now-idle van, looking at the building through the van's windows. The man on the passenger side smoked a cigarette and exhaled gray smoke out the slightly open window, although most of it remained inside, circling above his head. The driver appeared to be irritated and annoyed.

"Next time you decide to smoke, I am going to ask you to get the fuck out of the van," he scolded his companion. "You are suffocating me!"

His companion continued to smoke. He took another deep puff, inhaling smoke into his lungs, and tossed what remained of the cigarette out the window.

"Relax, boss," he said. "There are more polluted things out there that will kill you first." Smoke came out of his nostrils as he spoke. "Smog, congestion, crime-ridden streets, an irate car driver, an unlucky turn at the corner—my smoking should be at the bottom of things for you to worry about." He was in his twenties, with long black hair and thick eyebrows; he wore a t-shirt with a rock-star imprint and a snug pair of black jeans. He tilted his head backwards to pull back a shoulder-length strand of hair that had slipped in front of his right eye. His name was Nabeel, and he worked at a newspaper company. The driver was in his early forties, with gray sprouting everywhere in his full head of hair. His name was Jamaal, but every one called him J.D.

"How about we talk about this, boss?" Nabeel straightened his hair one more time and inhaled empty air. He leaned forward and gazed one more time at the building. "What are we doing here at this rundown place anyway?"

The rustic metal board with almost faded paint in front of the building read, "Marie Adelaide Rehabilitation Center."

"This is a drop center for street urchins with substance abuse issues," J.D. replied.

"You mean a shelter for drug junkies?"

"You could say that," J.D. answered. "The majority of the addicts who come here are street children. Here they find rehabilitation, food, hot water for bathing, and clean clothes."

"That is all good and noble, but what is our business here?" Nabeel sounded unimpressed.

"This place might give us a lead for the story. Almost all of the children murdered were urchins, runaways. I am sure quite a few of them came here for help at one point or another. I think we can gather useful information and might find some important clue," J.D. explained.

"Let's go in then, and see what's in store for us," Nabeel replied sarcastically. "I hope it will be warmer inside than out here in this cold."

The men exited the van and walked toward the building. The front door opened into a hallway, semi-illuminated by the smog-filled daylight. The hall was narrow and led to a white counter at the far end of its path. There were bulletin boards on the walls on both sides, along with doors to other rooms. The air inside smelled of ammonia, ether, and disinfectant. Both men walked toward the counter, casually examining the area, glancing into the open doors of rooms on each side. One of the rooms looked like a canteen, where a small crowd was gathered. They all seemed to be in a huddled position and were talking in whispers. Some of them noticed the passing shadows in the hallway and hushed others.

J.D. and Nabeel stopped at the counter. Nabeel raised himself on his toes to peek at the back room, which appeared to have shelving units placed against the wall. A tall man, rough-skinned and unshaven, emerged from the back.

"Yes?" he eyed both men and asked. He was a young man, but his weathered appearance showed that his years had taken a toll on him. His hair was snow white, his eyes pale, and his skin malnourished. A deep scar ran down from his left ear and vanished into the back of his neck. He could not have been more than twenty-five years old.

J.D. introduced himself and Nabeel and asked if he could talk to a supervisor for some information.

"What kind of information?" the inquisitive tone in the man's voice was obvious.

"I'm not sure if you are aware of the missing urchins."

"I pay close attention to the news."

"So—" J.D. started to speak.

"Are you the police?" the man behind the counter interrupted.

"No."

"Relative of one of the missing?"

"Not exactly," J.D. clarified.

"Then what is your business?"

"We just need to talk to someone about an ongoing investigative report." J.D. flashed his credentials. The young man grabbed the press ID from J.D, and looked at it closely.

"What do you want to know?" He turned the ID over a couple of times and handed it back.

"Anything on any of missing children who disappeared."

"You want to know if any of them are actually missing, or gone?"

"What do you mean?" J.D. asked.

"They are not missing if they are dead," the man said. "You have come here to know if they are actually dead?"

"Look, we just need to speak to someone for a few minutes about the whereabouts of street children who come to this place."

"I am the shift manager here. I am not sure if I can help you."

"I thought you said you kept abreast of the news," Nabeel said.

The man tensed. His facial expression changed.

"You are wasting your time being here," he said.

"We are trying to gather any information that might be helpful in capturing the killer who is on the loose."

"What makes you think we have any such information to provide? You know, we don't want any trouble with the law."

"Trust us. We are not police. Any information we get will be strictly confidential and for our investigation only," Nabeel assured him.

"Maybe you can give me your contact information. I will have my supervisor contact you when he comes in."

A shadow of disappointment ran across J.D.'s face.

"Are you sure there is no one else we can speak to right now?" He had heard that brush-off excuse many times in his career. The majority of people seemed to be afraid of sharing any information with the media or the police. They were hesitant to have their name associated with testimonies and thus exposing themselves to reprisals and police harassment.

The young man shrugged his shoulders.

J.D. handed him his card. Both men turned and started to walk away. Halfway down the hallway, a voice behind them halted their steps. Another man had appeared behind the counter. A little apprehensively he said, "My name is Constantine Ahuja. Let's talk."

Constantine ushered J.D. and Nabeel into the canteen and offered tea.

"I realize my colleague earlier was somewhat rude to you," he said to them. Constantine was a thirty-year-old man with a round face, split chin, and flat nose. "Surely you can understand his hesitance about being involved with the press, or police," he continued.

J.D. nodded.

"What made you approach us?" Nabeel asked after taking the cup of tea from him. "I am sure you heard our conversation at the counter."

Steam from the hot tea danced in front of Constantine's nose as he tilted the cup to take a sip. His eyes twitched as he gazed in the direction of his guests.

"I knew some of the victims." He put the cup on a side table. "It hurts to think what happened to them."

He had gained J.D. and Nabeel's undivided attention.

"Are you close to the urchins who come in for help?" J.D. asked.

"Some of them, yes."

"Do you think most of them are aware of what has been reported in the news?"

"It's hard to say; no one is talking," Constantine replied.

"What was your reaction to the news?" J.D, asked, as he took out a pen and a small notepad.

"Shocked, but not surprised," Constantine answered.

"Meaning?"

Outside, two children ran down the hallway, laughing loudly. A man yelled from one of the adjacent rooms and asked them to be less rowdy.

"Shocked that a crime of this magnitude took place; not surprised that, allegedly, one hundred urchins got kidnapped and no one raised an eyebrow."

A whiff of ether, sweet and nauseating, entered Nabeel's nose. He rose and opened a nearby window that faced the front yard to breathe in fresh air.

"How did you know the missing urchins? Can you describe them?" J.D scribbled on the notepad.

Constantine leaned back into his chair and pondered for a few seconds.

"Runaways, ten to thirteen years in age, average street urchins found working on the street, or begging for leftover food outside the restaurants, living in packs." He looked up at the ceiling when he spoke.

"So there was nothing about them that might have separated them from other urchins?"

Constantine tilted his head back down and looked deep into J.D.'s eyes. Nabeel closed the window and sat back down.

"No one deserves to die this way." The friendly tone in his voice had vanished.

"What?" J.D. sounded surprised.

"Are you asking me if any of the victims acted in a certain way to deserve what they got?"

"That is not ... I am sorry," J.D mumbled.

"You want to know if they had it coming?"

"No, I—" the words stumbled out of J.D.'s mouth.

"Did they?" Nabeel interrupted.

Constantine shifted his gaze toward Nabeel. Cold shadows of anger and scornfulness moved on his face.

"Have you ever lived on the street?" he asked.

"Can't say that I have." Nabeel put a toothpick between his lips.

"Then you are not aware of what a day in the life of a street urchin is like, do you?"

Nabeel shifted his weight on the chair. An uneasy feeling crawled inside him.

"I was there," Constantine continued. "I know what it is like sleeping in the park or under a bridge, being picked up by the police, scorned by the public, your hard-earned wage snatched by someone stronger than you." Constantine spat saliva as he spoke. His face had turned red. "I was one of them once." Constantine cleared his throat. "Just like them, I was a street urchin, a drug addict, brutalized and abused day in and day out."

Constantine got up and took a seat by the window. The sunlight made a halo around his head.

"And then to wake up the next morning and do it all over again, to let yourself be at the mercy of the dangers lurking out there, I know it all too well," he said. "I know the life they live, and many times what they think. I am sure so many of them walking the streets today knew at least one of the hundred children reported missing. And they all talk among themselves. It's a tight circle for street urchins. There is not much of a support system out there for them except for each other. I can see apprehension in their eyes when they come in, the fear of not knowing how or why it happened. They come in, get what they need, and leave, quietly."

The air filled with silence. J.D.'s mouth half opened to apologize one more time, but he repressed the urge.

"Maybe some of them sniffed glue, visited brothels, tried to steal and got caught. Maybe their behavior exposed them to more danger, maybe it didn't." Constantine's breathing had gotten heavier. "Despite what they got themselves into, none of them deserved to die the way they did."

"Do you think some of them who visit this center might want to talk to us?" J.D. asked, his tone empathetic and friendly.

"I am not sure" Constantine replied, now calm. "Trust is a big issue for these children."

"We would really like to have a chat with them, if you are willing to help us," J.D. said.

Constantine promised he would point out some of the regulars when they came in. "But approaching them and trying to talk to them will be entirely up to you."

J.D. and Nabeel shook hands with Constantine. On their way out, they passed a fair- skinned, green-eyed, blond teenager. Jogi walked straight over to the counter and greeted Constantine.

8 THE KILLER

December 10, 1999

Ghurki was a sleepy little village on the outskirts of Lahore, adjacent to the border with India. Its population was fewer than four thousand. Narrow streets led to houses made of bricks and plaster, sporadically laid out around the village. Unpaved dusty paths around the bend of a canal gave way to fields of corn, potatoes, and rice. People used bicycles as their main mode of transportation. Farmers, cobblers, masons, and merchants lived simple, modest, peaceful lives. Civil disputes were resolved quickly between families, usually ending with a handshake.

It was an early morning hour like many in the past. Households woke up to the sound of *azaan* (the call for morning prayers). Roosters crowed at dawn, announcing the arrival of another day. Dark windows lighted around the neighborhood as mothers got busy in their kitchens preparing meals for their husbands and children. All looked and felt the same. Little did they know that all was not the same. There was someone among them that morning, lying on a bed in a not-too-distant hotel. He was not one of them. As doors opened and men left their houses to earn a living, they did not know who that stranger was, one who had appeared like a shadow in the velvety blackness of the night. When he sat at the farthest, least-visible corner of the restaurant and ate alone, some wondered where he had come from. Others questioned his manners when he did not respond to their greetings.

The room at the hotel was dark. With his hand placed on his chest, his eyes gazing at the ceiling, he lay motionless in bed, like a corpse inside a casket. A musky wind blew occasionally through the cracked window, rumpling the dark drapes drawn closed, perturbing the still silence. It was on the news. At the front desk, while checking in the night before, he had caught a glimpse of it on the grainy, blurred screen of a badly tuned television set. Through the fading sound and picture of weak reception he could hear snippets. Attempts by the registration clerk to adjust the reception did not help either. But he knew all too well what the news was all about. It was just as he had envisioned: a freak show.

His still body gave the impression of a statue lying on the bed. But his brain raced through the years that had led him to where he was today. In the rustled silence he could hear his heart pounding behind his rib cage. There was nothing unusual about why he had picked Ghurki as a refuge.

He recalled being here before with his father and five brothers. Ghurki was vacation destination for the family. Every year, he remembered, they drove there in a large van and spent one week of the hunting season there. He was a little boy back then, only nine.

It was here he was called *gandu* for the first time in his life. In his early years, he did not understand the meaning of that word very well. Those he asked did not answer. It had been during one of those hunting trips that he had first heard it. He recalled walking alongside his father amid wheat fields, with the crop taller than he.

His brothers had spread out across the field, looking for unsuspecting prey. He, on the other hand, chose to stick close to his father. It was a warm summer day. The sky was clear and the early morning fresh breeze was giving way to increasingly hot and humid air. Though excited about the hunting trip, his heart wasn't into it. It wasn't long before he found himself wandering away from the hunting team.

Unaware of the slowly approaching hunters, a shy deer picked a spot under the shade of a willow tree to keep himself cool from the sweltering heat. Moments before the fingers would have pressed on triggers and fired, a loud scream filled the air, startling everyone—including the deer, who jumped to his feet and galloped into the nearby forest. Everyone ran in the direction of the scream. About three hundred yards north, beyond the wild bushes, they found Javed captured by two men. A little boy with scared looks and a scratched face tried to hide behind one of the men. The man holding Javed jerked him around as the boy tried to free himself from the man's grip.

"Does this boy belong to you?" the man holding Javed inquired of the oncoming men in an anguished tone.

Peasants working nearby stopped to look at what was going on. Upon inquiry from his father, he was told that Javed had sat on the boy's chest and banged his head against the ground.

"He called me *gandu*!" Javed cried.

Later that night, Javed told his father that the young boy attended the same *madrasa* Javed did to learn the Quran while he vacationed in Ghurki. Flushed, he also told his father that the boy had seen him and the *madrasa* teacher together alone in a room.

"What are you talking about?"

Javed leaned over and whispered in his father's year. Javed's father's eyes widened as he pushed Javed away. He shook Javed by his shoulders and asked that he repent right away.

Then they all packed in a hurry and got back in the van to go back to the city.

"What is a *gandu*?" Javed asked his father as they took off. In response, his father pulled over to the side and slapped him across the face, his body trembling with anger.

Over the years he heard himself being called *gandu* several times. But by then he wasn't looking for the meaning. His family went back to Ghurki every year. And while on vacation, Javed attended the same *madrasa* and was left alone in the room with the same *madrasa* teacher. He realized the meaning of the word eventually: a submissive, passive giver, willing to be taken by a man. Javed never repeated what happened at the *madrasa* to his father.

He had heard himself being called that name over the years, people quipping and smirking as he walked by. And there was the woman who had approached him in the market square and thrown a shoe at him: "Leave us alone, you *gandu*!" she screamed. And a night when the two urchin boys he had hired for a massage had beaten him mercilessly and left him almost dead. With each blow, he had heard them laugh and call him *gandu*. He remembered when his family had refused to let him see his dying father and had slammed the door on him, calling him names he had grown accustomed to.

The bed made a crackling noise as he shifted his weight. In the dark hotel room, his mind was talking to itself. He had finished what he had set out to do. Yet his mind was restless. He should have been at peace after achieving his own justice against the society that had so blatantly let him down. Yet he could not fall asleep. Javed shook his head.

He could not claim victory entirely to himself. The game was made too easy for him. They were all such easy prey, he thought. Why did no one come looking for them? But wasn't that exactly the point he wanted to prove: that for some, life has very little value? So many can be taken from the streets of a bustling city, and no one will notice? He had proved it one hundred times, right?

Or was it the sheer agony of revenge? He grabbed his head. Why were his thoughts getting so complicated? Had the long-ago senseless beating by the two homeless urchins driven him over the edge? He sat up and moved to edge of the bed. As calm as the air was around him, the space inside his mind was howling with voices piercing his brain like shards of glass. He took another look back into his childhood. Was it because he had stopped talking about it, about Ghurki, about the *madrasa* and the *madrasa* teacher? He grunted as he got up and paced swiftly around the room.

Another wave of memory came crashing in. He recalled the sense of adrenaline rush mixed in with the fear of being caught the first time. How good it had felt to do it. No one called him *gandu* afterwards, he noticed. No one came looking for the missing. No one knocked on the door or inquired. Soon it became routine. How ordinary it became, to take a life. He became God. Shortly thereafter, it was merely to achieve inner satisfaction. The thrill and rush was gone. But he needed an audience, someone to admire his work. Did they think it was easy to do what he had accomplished, taking one hundred lives to teach society a lesson? Javed slammed his fist on the nightstand next to the bed.

He had orchestrated it flawlessly, had made them vanish into thin air, dumping their remains into the river after dissolving them in a vat of acid. Yes, he had had assistance, but he was the brain behind it all. Yet no one got up and clapped at the final act when the curtain went down. They had deserted him in this lifetime, but his name was sure to go down in history. Those who had called him *gandu* would drop their jaws. He had given them something they were sure to remember for the rest of their lives. He felt laughter erupting through his lungs.

It was nothing short of masterwork to walk among them and take them one by one till the very last one, all one hundred of them, to be the fuel for his raging desire and revenge. Silence shattered as his laughter roared in the air. He stood in the middle of the room, eyes closed, arms spread in the shape of a Y.

He tried to picture the looks on their faces when they read the letter he'd sent to the police. His left foot took one step back, as if getting ready to dance. Did they laugh, did they believe it? He cocked his head and wondered.

One step forward, right foot up, then he was dancing. What was it like for them entering the house without him being there? He pictured the wall covered with photos, the bloodstains, the journal, the vat with bones on top. It was as if he had been in the room with them when the press and the police had swarmed in. They could not see him, but he was standing in a corner, watching them take pictures and collect evidence. He pictured one police officer throw up when he opened the lid to the vat. With every news story, with every detail reported in the paper, his imagination took him right back to 167 Ravi Road.

Javed was swinging around the room now. He laughed at their sealed lips and utter disbelief. Yes, how gratifying it was to picture that. The howling voices inside his mind intensified. He circled and then plopped back into bed, smiling. He opened his eyes and said out loud, "But the finale is yet to come." He chuckled and clapped the palms of his hands together.

. . .

January 1, 2000

The rain would not stop. A heavy downpour had continued for the past two days, drenching every inch of the city. It was unusually damp and dreary for this time of year. Birds on trees sat quietly with their heads down, wings soaked. Stray dogs tried to find shelter and were shooed off.

Cars splashing water drove through flooded streets. Raw, damp cold seemed to have gotten inside one's bones, refusing to leave. People indoors cranked up the heat on tea kettles and sat by the windows watching the continuous downpour.

Jogi lay inside the Ring by the river. The arched, gray ceiling of the sewage pipe had leaked, and water was dripping in. The air was filled with the sound of pounding rain and the white noise of the tires driving over the wet bridge. Jogi had caught a glimpse of himself in a mirror the other day. The person he saw there scared him: pale skin, dark circles under his eyes, and protruding bones on his face. Like a deflated balloon, life was slowly being sucked out of him, it seemed. He was diligent about taking the medication received from the rehab center, but that didn't seem to be working any more. He thought it won't be long now before the gang stops giving me the respect I've earned over the years. Why would anyone want to listen to a sick, skeleton-shaped gang leader who might blow away in a gust of wind?

Jogi wasn't his name when he was growing up in the streets of Kabul. His parents named him Barkat Ullah. They told him his name meant "God's blessing." By the time he was born and opened his eyes on the world in 1984, Afghanistan was already five years into the war against the Soviet Union. A bomb had exploded at the Kabul international airport on the day of his birth, killing and wounding several hundred people. He learned to walk and speak amid air assaults, reverberating gunfire, and Kabul radio claiming success against the Mujahidin.

Far on the horizon, past dusty unpaved roads and murky desert air, the striking peaks of Tora Bora and the Hindu Kush mountains thrust toward the sky and could be seen from where he grew up. At age six Barkat Ullah played in a playground that held a rusty, metal carcass of a broken-down Soviet tank. He climbed up the treeless ridges and played hide and seek behind the mud, stone, and brick-walled huts.

His father, a Tajik, was a merchant and sold women's clothes sewn by his wife. He was a tall, clean-shaven man with deep blue eyes and copper-toned skin. Every day after school, Barkat Ullah went straight to the shop and helped his father. He did his homework and at intervals took down show-cased dresses for inquiring customers, mostly women in burqas.

The war had ended and the Soviets had retreated, leaving behind the ravaged ruins of the royalist era of Zahir Shah, former king of Afghanistan. Barkat Ullah overheard his father one day talking to the neighboring shopkeeper, a mason. They were discussing the political uncertainty in the region caused by the feeble government of Dr. Najibullah, the former head of the Afghan intelligence agency. Barkat Ullah ran out to get some tea at his father's instruction.

"Your son is growing taller than the mountain behind him, Wazir *Agha* (mister)," Azim Ali said to Barkat Ullah's father, taking tea from the boy. "It is a good thing you don't have to worry about him being sent to Russia by the Soviets anymore." He ran his hand over Barkat Ullah's head with affection. "May a better life await you in the future."

Barkat Ullah sat on the window ledge while the two elders continued their discussion.

"There is news from the south of a new movement rising in Kandahar," Azim Ali, an Uzbek, said to Wazir Ullah.

"What type of movement?"

"My cousin who lives there has told me that Mujahidin have taken over Kandahar and are working to form a group called the Taliban."

"Taliban?"

The shopkeeper explained that the group consisted mainly of Mujahidin's orphan children, who had been sent to *madrasa*s in Pakistan and were now returning to take hold.

In April of 1992, the Mujahidin took aim at the city of Kabul. It marked the beginning of a three-year-long civil war.

Barkat Ulllah remembered the day when he heard the howling voices coming from the neighboring house. His mother hurriedly donned her burqa, grabbed his hand and stepped out to see the neighbor. They walked through the rubble, covering their faces and trying not to inhale dust and debris. The thunderous sound of an artillery attack roared at a distance. The year was 1994, and Hykamtyar's attack on Kabul had intensified. The ground rumbled as another rocket exploded high above a hill. Barkat Ullah's mother tugged him closer and ran.

She rushed through the neighbor's door, dragging him behind her. In the veranda on a *charpoy* lay the body of the neighbor's daughter, nine-year-old Abida. Only her head was visible from the white sheet that covered her. Several women were gathered around the *charpoy*, weeping and beating their chests. Barkat Ullah's mother covered his eyes as a warm wind blew and slid the sheet off Abida. Through the small opening between his mother's fingers, Barkat saw that below the torso Abida had no body left. She had been in a bazaar when a rocket had hit and killed several civilians, including her. Her mother fainted and fell to the floor.

By late 1996, with military support from Pakistan and financial backing from Saudi Arabia, the Taliban took control of Kabul and declared victory. Late one September afternoon, on his way to the shop after school, twelve-year-old Barkat Ullah saw three men gathered in front of the shop, talking to his father. He hurried. The men were wearing turbans, had full-grown beards, and were carrying rifles. Their voices got louder as Barkat Ullah got closer. They were asking Wazir Ullah if he was a Tajik.

"It is the *sharia* (Islamic law) and *sunnah* (Muhammadic practice)," one of the men said loudly.

Another man stepped inside the shop and walked out carrying a woman's dress. It was a knee-length *kameez*, embroidered with a yellow border and with red, black, and blue stripes.

"I am a God-fearing man and know my faith," Wazi Ullah said, his face tense and his eyes staring into space.

"Then you must know all men of God must follow *sunnah* and grow a beard."

The wind was blowing in his direction, and Barkat Ullah could hear the men clearly. His heart pounded as he raced toward them. This was the first time he had seen Taliban men walking through the bazaar, the ones he had heard his father talk about.

"What is your business selling women's clothes?" The man holding the *kameez* waved it in the air and used an accusatory tone.

"That is how I make my living. I am an honest family man." Wazir Ullah tried to remain calm.

"In this time of chaos and anarchy, we are your hope to bring peace and order to this land, to give people what they deserve: the word of God and his will. It is long overdue." The older of the three, a man with a gray beard, placed his hand on

Wazir Ullah's shoulder. Barkat Ullah stood by his father's side and watched the men leave.

"Change is coming, *bacha*." His father gazed at the settling dust cloud behind the Taliban men's jeep, his right arm around Barkat Ullah's shoulder. "Change is upon us."

They decided to flee Kabul to avoid strict draconian decrees. Wazir Ullah arranged for a pick-up truck to transport his family up north. Barkat Ullah remembered his father consoling him for leaving Kabul. He also remembered the night his father spoke his last words in his arms.

Three days prior to their departure, Barkat Ullah's mother went out to the neighbor's house to ask for some rice. His father was busy inside the room, packing and listening to radio Kabul. Barkat Ullah sat in the veranda on a pile of blankets tied by a rope that were ready to be moved. A dusty old Russian book lay by his side. He tore pages from the book and made moth-shaped paper planes with each page. He carefully folded the page in half the long way, folded each top corner toward the center, turned the page over onto the other side and folded it in half, and finally folded both wings so the outside edge could run parallel to the body. Some planes dove, some climbed and crashed. He held a few in his hand and pranced around, comparing them to the real warplanes he had grown accustomed to over the years. It took a few tries before he made the perfect plane. He slightly angled the rear of the wing down, blew air into the middle, and threw it in the air. The plane glided in a perfect straight motion toward the door. As Barkat Ullah watched in amazement, the plane fluttering up and down in the wind, the door slammed opened and a few strange men wearing turbans entered the house. His mother, right behind, was being pulled by her hair by one of the men. The paper plane landed and was crushed under the feet of the intruders.

Barkat Ullah's scream made his father rush out. He recognized them immediately. They were part of the *munkrat* (religious Taliban police). At his leader's nod, the man holding Barkat Ullah's mother let go of her hair, dropping her on the floor. Wazir Ullah shouted and asked what she had done wrong.

"The face of a woman is a source of lust," said the leader out loud. He was wearing a gray vest and a black turban and had a white beard.

Wazir Ullah tried to reach for his wife, but was pushed to the side. The leader of the *munkrat* was reciting the decree, as if reading them their rights.

Women of the household were not to step outside their house, Wazir Ullah heard him say. They were to cover themselves and be accompanied by a man from the household if they did go out. Outside the house, they were not to wear makeup or jewelry or appear in front of men not related to them.

Earlier that morning, Wazir Ullah had stood behind his wife while she was braiding her long hair. "I have not seen you in these in such a long time," he whispered, as he produced a pair of earrings he had bought for her at a fair a few years back. She smiled, flushed slightly, and agreed to wear them.

Wazir Ullah did not know the earrings would serve as the death warrant for his wife. She had been found by the *munkrat* receiving a bowl of rice from the neighbor's eighteen-year-old son, smiling, uncovered, and flaunting shimmering jewelry, the leader told Wazir Ullah.

They covered her face with a sack. Two men grabbed her by the ankles, placed her hands behind her back so she would not fight back, and laid her with her back flat on the floor. Holding an oiled wooden stick, the leader crouched next to her.

"Forgive me, *hamsheera* (sister)," he jeered in her covered ear. "But law and order must be restored," He raised the stick and struck her stomach. She cried out in pain. Wazir Ullah rushed to lie over her and cover her. One of the standing men jabbed a rifle butt into his left temple. A fountain of blood erupted. Wazir Ullah staggered and walked a few feet toward Barkat Ullah. The stick beating continued. During one strike, the mother raised her head in pain and when it dropped back down, she struck a protruding brick on the floor. She became nonresponsive to the beating after that. When they removed the sack from her face a few minutes later, blood was seeping from the back of her head, pooling around the earrings still in her ears.

"What about the boy?" one of the men asked his leader on their way out.

The leader took one good look at Barkat Ullah. "Leave him."

Barkat Ullah sat on the floor and held his father's blood-covered head in his lap. A few feet away, his mother's body lay motionless. With a finger motion, Wazir Ullah asked his son to lean over. His lips touching his son's ear, Wazir Ullah whispered, "This is not the life I envisioned for you my son. Please forgive me." Barkat Ullah held his father tight.

"You must leave Kabul, *bacha*," he said, with slowly departing breaths. "Go to Spin Buldak on the border and find your uncle, Amir Khan. Ask him to take you to the city of Chaman in Pakistan." He gasped for air. Barkat Ullah's tears fell on his face. "A better life awaits you, *bacha*, on the other side of the mountain. They will come back soon, *meri jaan* (my soul). Don't let them find you. Leave me here and go now." Even in his dying moments Wazir Ullah was aware of Afghan tradition. Sons of the deceased were to be the pallbearers and were responsible for taking their parents to their graves. He knew Barkat Ullah could have been persuaded easily to carry out family tradition and pride.

"Your mother and I will look upon you from afar and send prayers for your safety from harm's way. But you must leave, *bacha*. You must go."

Barkat Ullah cradled his father's head long after he had closed his eyes. His chest slowly deflated. Sometime in the middle of the night, Wazir Ullah stopped breathing. In those wee hours of the morning, Barkat Ullah packed a small bag with two pieces of clothing and a piece of bread, and left the house for Spin Buldak.

Amir Khan, his father's younger brother, received Barkat Ullah with open arms and teary eyes. Amir Khan's wife and two daughters made him a comfortable bed on a *charpoy* with clean sheets and a blanket. At night they offered him wheat bread and spinach cooked in butter cream. Glowing embers of burning wood reflected on Barkat Ullah's face as he sat on the floor and ate with his head down. Amir Khan's daughters watched him from the window of an adjacent room.

After dinner, Amir Khan came in to the room and sat beside him on the *charpoy*.

"You have traveled far, son. You must rest well," Amir Khan said. Barkat Ullah conveyed his deceased father's last words.

"I am obligated to carry out my brother's last wishes," Amir Khan said. "But you must stay here for a few days and gather your strength."

"Have you travelled to the other side, *Agha*?" Barkat Ullah asked.

"Yes, I have."

Barkat Ullah asked what it was like there.

"It is peaceful," Amir Khan responded. "They are all friends. I'll make sure you are in good hands once you cross the border."

Barkat Ullah spent the next couple weeks with Amir Khan's family. He helped Amir Khan cut down an old willow tree, chopped wood and hauled fire logs, cleaned his uncle's bicycle, brought him lunch at work, and watched barefoot boys play soccer with a half-deflated ball. He practiced his homework, the last one he remembered, over and over again.

"Practice makes it perfect," he remembered his teacher saying once. He borrowed a notebook and drew mountains, a sun-filled sky with birds flying, and his house. One day, Amir Khan's wife Rizwana walked into the room and found Barkat Ullah lamenting. She slowly walked over and sat by him.

"What is the matter, *bacha*?" she asked.

"I can't remember them," Barkat Ullah sniffed. "I can't remember my parents' faces."

"It's okay." She held him by the shoulder and drew him closer.

"How can I forget them so soon?"

"You have not, I assure you."

"Then why can't I see their faces when I think of them?" Barkat Ullah asked.

"You must think of them in a moment," she said. "A happy moment, that is, and it will all be clear to you. Think of a time you spent with them that you cherish, and their images will never leave your mind."

That night Barkat Ullah dreamt about his parents. They were in the room, standing around the *charpoy*, gazing at him compassionately.

The following day, Amir Khan asked him to stay when he brought over lunch to the shop.

"There is someone I want you to meet."

Toward evening, when the shadows grew taller, a man came into the shop. He was a gray-haired man with a trim beard and a big spiky nose. He sat next to Barkat Ullah.

"This is Sajid Khan," Amir introduced the man to Barkat Ullah. "He will take you across the border to Pakistan."

"Will you go with me?" Barkat Ullah asked Amir Khan.

"I would love to, *bacha*, but I have a family matter to take care of. Besides, Sajid Khan is a personal friend, and I have his guarantee you will be safe."

"No need to worry, son. I will make sure you reach your destination safe and sound," Sajid

Khan said in a hoarse voice. He coughed as he spoke.

"I have arranged for you to be admitted to a *madrasa* in Chaman. There are other boys who live there, so you won't feel alone. You will be in good hands and receive a good education, I am sure." Amir Khan placed his hands on Barkat Ullah's head affectionately.

"Will I ever come back, *Agha*?"

"I am sure. You are an Afghan, my son, a Tajik at heart. Once you have a wealth of knowledge and all the skills of becoming a man, I am certain you will find your way back home."

Barkat Ullah asked when he would have to leave.

"Tomorrow morning. There is a bus that leaves for Chaman at four. You must board the bus with Sajid Khan."

Barkat Ullah spent his last night in Afghanistan lying awake, wondering what it would be like tomorrow. The thrill of a journey to another country and nervousness about an unknown world kept him up. He finally got up two hours before the scheduled departure, washed his face, and put on a brown-and-red plaid shirt and black trousers. He then sat on the *charpoy* with his bag in his lap and waited. Rizwana packed him *dahl* and *halva* (a sweet) for the road.

Sajid Khan knocked on the door half an hour before the departure. While Amir Khan chatted with Sajid Kahn outside, Barkat Ullah said his goodbyes to Rizwana. The little girls looked on from the bedroom windows and waved. Barkat Ullah thanked them for their hospitality. As he walked out to join the men, he glimpsed Amir Khan sliding something into his pocket.

Burqa-clad women, children with runny noses, and live poultry packed in wooden crates crowded the bus. The bus driver sat at the nearby café and sipped tea while the bus loaded. Barkat Ullah took a window seat and Sajid Khan sat next to him. Amir Khan stood outside and smoked a cigarette. He gave occasional uneasy glances at Barkat Ullah.

"You will be okay, *bacha*," Amir Khan assured him.

"I will be okay."

"Just be brave; no matter what happens, be strong." Amir Khan sauntered along as the bus started to pull out. Barkat Ullah waved through the window, and Amir Khan motioned back. Soon he disappeared behind the dust and black smoke as the bus took off.

At the border, Barkat Ullah repeated under his breath what he had been instructed by Sajid Khan to say. If asked, he was Sajid Khan's nephew going to visit his stricken grandmother in Chaman. Through the dust-coated window, Barkat Ullah watched Sajid Khan talking to the patrol agent. Sajid shook his head and smiled sheepishly. The patrol officer walked over to the window and gazed at Barkat Ullah intently. They were allowed to pass.

"This is Tariq," Sajid Khan introduced a man to Barkat Ullah as they were sitting at a cafeteria eating *naan* and mutton cooked in ginger, lemon, and tomato paste. Right after arriving at Chaman, Sajid Khan had hurriedly boarded another bus. He had walked fast and almost dragged Barkat Ullah through the crowd. Soon they were on their way to Peshawar. Barkat Ullah sat quietly and followed the lead of a stranger he hadn't gotten the chance to know very well. Upon arrival he marveled at the hustle and bustle of the city: the crowded *Chowk Yaadgar* (Square of Remembrance), the busy storefronts of Saddar Road, and the historic Khyber Pass left him speechless. It was nothing like the war-torn Kandahar and Kabul he had left behind. Barkat Ullah wished his parents were here with him instead of Sajid Khan.

"Are you hungry, *bacha*?" Sajid Khan's voice startled him. He nodded. The bus was pulling into a narrow bus depot.

"Me, too," Sajid Khan acknowledged.

They walked across the street and entered a bazaar inside a cobblestone street. Faded store signs covered by tin awnings were on both sides. People went about their business. The sound of *Pushto* (one of the official languages of Afghanistan) music coming from a tape recorder perched on the window of a store shattered the already clamor-saturated air.

"Stay close to me at all times," Sajid Khan told Barkat Ullah.

The man introduced as Tariq had a long, thick moustache that was twisted on the ends, and a large mole right below his nose. He sat across from Barkat Ullah and sipped *kahwa* (green tea). He asked Sajid Khan about the trip while darting glances at Barkat Ullah from the corner of his eye. The men exchanged small talk while Barkat Ullah splurged on a freshly cooked meal. The aroma of food, rising from an adjacent restaurant, had made him famished. When he looked up, the two men were smoking cigarettes and drinking tea.

"Did you like the food, *bacha*?" Sajid Khan addressed Barkat Ullah.

"It was tasty," Barkat Ullah replied.

"Good. Now listen carefully. Tariq is a friend, and he is here to take you."

"Where will he take me?" Barkat Ullah asked in an alarmed voice.

"You are to go to Rawal Pindi with him," Sajid Khan replied.

"Is it where the *madrasa* is where I am supposed to go to school?"

"You must listen to Tariq at all times, and do as he says."

"What about you, Sajid *Agha*?" Barkat Ullah asked. "Will you come with me?"

"No, my job to bring you here is done."

"I don't want to go to Rawal Pindi," Barkat Ullah winced.

"You have to go with Tariq now." Sajid Khan crushed his cigarette butt under his shoes.

"But Amir *Agha* told me I will live in Chaman." Barkat Ullah's lips quivered.

"Enough!" Tariq scolded from across the table, jolting Barkat Ullah. "This is not Chaman. You are not in Afghanistan anymore. You do as you are told. We did not pay thousands for some whining wimp," he sneered. "The free meal is over, boy."

Tariq kicked the chair and dragged Barkat Ullah onto his feet. "Now let's go. I don't have all day." On their way out of the bazaar, Barkat Ullah turned to look back. But Sajid Khan had already disappeared in the crowd.

The next bus ride ended at Pir Wadhai, a major bus station depot surrounded by open sewers, workshops, vegetable stalls, and many small hotels serving passengers in transit. Tariq took Barkat Ullah through inner streets to the Paramount Hotel. It was an old, two-story building with chipped plaster and molded window shutters. Rooms for rent were upstairs and a restaurant was on the first floor. The restaurant owner was a scruffy-looking old man. His eyes brightened when he saw Barkat Ullah.

"What have you got for me there, Tariq Khan?" he exclaimed from across the table.

"Just arrived from across the border; thought I would pay you a visit," Tariq responded with a grin.

"Green eyes and yellow hair in the midst of all the browns and blacks, you know my business too well." The manager's gaze bored into Barkat Ullah. "This will do wonders."

"You expect the best, and I deliver."

"You certainly do, my friend, you certainly do."

Barkat Ullah was hired right away as help. He served at table and cleaned the floor. There were others working at the hotel like him. His distinct Afghani features—blonde hair, sparkling green eyes, and light skin—made him stand out in the crowd. The hotel was always crowded. Travelers switching buses to go to Swat and Kashmir, truck drivers stopping overnight to rest—the Paramount Hotel was a revolving door to all.

One late evening, the manager told Barkat Ullah to take *chai* (tea), to one of the rooms upstairs.

"He is a special guest. Make sure you are nice to him." He grabbed Barkat Ullah by the shoulder as he spoke. Barkat Ullah nodded and headed upstairs.

"Wait!" the manager called him back.

"You need to be presentable. Come sit here for a second so I can put some *surma* on you." Barkat Ullah sat silently and watched a metal needle slide across his eyes, spreading black eyeliner.

"And if someone asks, tell them your name is Jogi. No one wants service from someone named Barkat Ullah."

. . .

'A better life awaits you, *bacha*, on the other side of the mountain.' His father's last words echoed in his mind. Jogi's bones ached as he tried to shift his weight. The rain had stopped, and the dripping of rainwater from the leaky pipe had come to a gradual halt.

Barkat Ullah, now Jogi, had worked as an itinerant pleasure boy who lured travelers to come and stay at the Paramount Hotel. After six months, while attempting to lure a customer to the hotel, Jogi was dragged into a nearby deserted train yard. He had attacked his assailer with a brick and hopped on a passing freight train en route to Lahore.

Jogi stepped out and slowly climbed up to the bridge. The air was fresh and cold right after the rain. Rainwater dropped from leaves, occasionally landing on the necks of passersby and making them flinch. Avoiding the spread-out puddles on the road, Jogi walked west, leaving the crowd behind. He walked down long, narrow cobblestone streets that eventually ended at the back side of the railway station, where locomotives were brought in for repair and maintenance. Jogi walked along the long stretch of empty train cars brought in for repair. His steps were hesitant yet constant. He had promised himself never to take this trip. He recalled many other times he had stopped himself from going across the train yard to the other side. Times had changed. He was in pain, deteriorating from the inside, and as much as he detested it, there was no apparent other choice.

Jogi found an open car. He climbed in and walked out through the opposite door. It was hard to see through the dim light from the lamp posts. The shadows grew even darker where Jogi headed, further from the murky light. As he got closer, Jogi saw a narrow opening between two loading docks. Gingerly he entered. His nostrils instantly filled with the smell of urine and rusting metal. With squinted eyes, Jogi stepped forward and noticed moving figures, some crouched, others leaning against the wall. He walked among them as glares followed him. Someone grabbed his wrists and mumbled something. Jogi jerked his hands free and kept on walking. A hand on his shoulder brought him to a halt.

"Well, isn't this the messiah coming to visit us." Meera's voice entered Jogi's ears.

"Didn't expect to see you anytime soon after your last rescue mission."

Jogi felt Meera's breath on his neck.

"Did you forget your way around the city?" Meera snickered.

"I have come here to ask for your help."

"My help?" Meera got closer as he laughed. "I never thought I would hear these words."

"Believe me when I tell you. It is true." Jogi chewed the words, his voice weak.

"The green-eyed wonder don't look so marvelous anymore." Meera's face was inches from Jogi. "What is eating you, Jogi? You are paler than the yellow moon. What makes you think I will help you and not slit your throat?"

"Because I know you better. Killing me in cold blood won't give you the satisfaction. You'd rather watch me go down in front of everyone, one breath at a time. Tell me if I am wrong."

Meera circled around and sniffed Jogi. "You are quite perceptive. I like that about you. For all the pain you have caused me in the past, I would give anything to see you on your knees in front of me at the market square, begging for mercy."

Over the years, the rivalry between Jogi and Meera had grown stronger, each one the leader of their own gang living on opposite sides of the city. Upon his arrival in Lahore, Jogi had made his way to Data Baksh's shrine, dedicated to a Sufi saint who had brought Sufism and the spirit of brotherhood to the subcontinent. He waited in line with the pilgrims and devotees to get some *langar* (free food). Barefoot on the white marble floor of the courtyard outside the tomb, Jogi watched a devotee play the *dohl* (drum) hanging from his neck. He danced in circles and spun his long hair in trance. Later, while trying to find shelter for the night, he saw Meera sitting on the chest of a boy in a side alley. Meera banged the boy's head to the ground and shouted loudly.

Jogi had rescued the boy from Meera. That night he founded his own gang, consisting of the one boy he had just rescued. Both gangs avoided interaction by not mingling or intruding into each other's territory. One thing Meera's gang was known for was the rampant use of drugs. He encouraged and provided *hashish*, *ganja*, and glue to his group. At the end of each day he and his friends gathered in small, unnoticed alleys and shared yellow paper bags of sniffing glue. Jogi, on the other hand, prohibited the use of any kind of drugs among his gang. Occasionally one of them would be tempted to try a free sample offered by one of Meera's boys, but would be intercepted by Jogi just in time before they were addicted to it.

"Look at yourself!" Jogi had growled at Kamal, one of the boys he had found last summer intoxicated in the park. "You don't think life is rough enough for you?"

"Life is fucked up, and this is the solution to forget it all." The broken words spilled out of Kamal's mouth.

"And where will you go when it wears out, huh?" Jogi grabbed him by the collar.

"*Sala harami*! You're worried about tomorrow. I want to enjoy this moment, right here, right now. Leave me the fuck alone." Kamal swayed as he tried to walk away from Jogi. Jogi had had to carry him on his shoulders to the rehab center.

Jogi and Meera had clashed several times, and each time the resentment between the two had grown stronger. With the help of the rehab center, Jogi was able to eliminate many of the drug-dealing corners run by Meera and push them back into only one on the west side of the city.

"I do want to ask you this, though." Meera circled around Jogi. "Why the sudden desire to use?"

"To ease the pain. Nothing else seems to be working," Jogi replied.

"I am loving the irony in the situation," Meera hissed. "You have come to me to help you ease the pain, someone who wants nothing but to inflict it upon you."

"I thought you might find it poetic," Jogi said.

"It must be intense, the pain that is, not to care about how your gang will take it once they find out their leader is dealing."

"It is between you and me, no one else." Jogi's voice got tense. "You can kill me here, or I'll walk out if there is any doubt."

"Don't be so serious *dost* (friend). I never said I wouldn't give you what you seek. But that is not to say the situation cannot be taken advantage of.

You really didn't think you would get that for free, did you?"

"No, but I knew you wouldn't want to miss the opportunity."

"Indeed. As ironic as it sounds, helping you get loaded and watch you float will give me all the pleasure in the world." Meera motioned to one of his men, who brought over a small tin can.

"Special blend, glue mixed with ether and gasoline, just for you," Meera smiled.

"What do I owe you for this?" Jogi asked.

"Not to worry. Take this as a sample. We'll talk business next time when you return. And you will, I am sure," Meera smirked.

Jogi grabbed Meera by the back of his neck and said something in his ear before walking out.

"Follow him and report back his every move," Meera said to one of the boys as Jogi left, holding the tin can in his hand.

Jogi walked back toward the idle train cars, his hands shaking. He had walked into a lion's den and come back out alive. He had not told anyone where he was going. Meera could have killed him, and his body would not have been found till weeks later. His fingers clutched the tin can, and he walked faster. He looked for a safe place to sit and sniff some glue. The faint sound of steps, crunching the old settled dust, entered his ears. A few yards behind, he noticed, someone was following him. Fear rushed through his veins. His first inclination led him to Meera. Maybe he hadn't been so lucky, he thought. Maybe it was Meera's way of deluding him into believing he was safe. Maybe he was right behind him about to stab him in the back. Jogi picked up his speed. In the utter silence of the night, he could hear his heart pounding. His legs started to stiffen. The shadows behind him were getting closer. He ran and leaped to jump over some train tracks. Missing by a few inches, he landed right in the middle. The tin can flew from his hand and slipped under one of the cars. His scream echoed in the vast, empty train yard. As Jogi struggled to get back on his feet, he realized it was too late. He turned to face his chasers. Two sets of eyes were staring at him intently.

. . .

J.D. and Nabeel sat across the table from Jogi at Café Pyala, sipping cups of tea.

"Sorry about the fall. Hope it doesn't hurt too much," J.D. addressed Jogi.

Jogi took a look at the bruised knee and slashed wrist.

"You could have simply called for me instead of running after me."

"We were afraid it might spook you," J.D. said.

Jogi reached over to the pack of cigarettes that belonged to Nabeel. After receiving a nod from Nabeel, he took one out and lit it.

"Tell me again who you are and why you were following me?" Jogi asked, as he inhaled the smoke and tilted his head backwards. J.D. told him they had spotted him at the rehab center.

"We just want to talk," J.D. said.

"No one talks to street urchins without a motive. What are you up to?"

"What can you tell us about the vanishings of one hundred street children?" Nabeel asked.

Jogi looked through the blowing gray smoke in front of him. Images of Daud, Raja, and Rehman appeared in his mind. That dreadful feeling, when he had stood outside the empty sewage pipes and wondered about the whereabouts of their occupants, crept back up.

"I have nothing to say about that," Jogi finally spoke, with a flat face. "And even if I did, what makes you so sure I'll share anything with you?"

"Because we think you cared about some of them There is a chance you stay up at nights and wonder how this could have happened under your watch. They looked to you for protection," Nabeel said.

Jogi winced and shifted his weight on the chair.

"Look, we are on your side. Talking to us might help some of the weight off your shoulders."

"Thanks for the offer, but I don't think you can help."

J.D. mentioned the connection between press and law enforcement and how it could help get to the killer.

"Police," Jogi snickered. "You don't know anything about the streets, do you?"

"Maybe today is the day we get to learn," Nabeel responded. "Tell us."

"The police are probably happy they have fewer street urchins to deal with," Jogi scoffed.

"A little exaggerated, but go on."

"You have not seen a runaway in the hands of the police. You have never sat back and watched a little boy being beaten by someone three times his size. You have not prowled the street in the dead of night and witnessed how we make it to the dawn. Unless you have lived through it, you will never know anything about me or any others like me." Jogi spat on the floor.

"Let's go, we are wasting our time with him." Nabeel crushed his cigarette butt under his shoe and got up. "Maybe one day, when you stop playing the victim card, you'll be able to distinguish between friend and foe," he said to Jogi.

"We know that you came here from Afghanistan." J.D. kept his composure despite Jogi's outburst.

"Ten points for making such an easy guess." Jogi pointed at his dusty blonde hair and green eyes.

"Your parents probably didn't make it as refugees, and you landed on the streets."

A noticeable shade of grief ran over Jogi's face. Having his parents mentioned took him back to the streets of Kabul.

"We also know that you are here illegally," Nabeel joined in.

"Are we correct so far?" J.D. asked.

"So what, you'll have me deported. Trust me, I won't be taking any fond memories of this place with me." Jogi pushed his back against the chair, took and lit another cigarette.

"We had a talk with Constantine at the rehab center," J.D. said. "We know why you are sick, Jogi. We can help you," J.D. responded. "And no one is going to send you back."

"Tell me what is wrong with me. The rehab center gives me pills, but won't say what I got."

Both men looked at each other. They finally had Jogi's attention.

"It goes back to your days at Pir Wadhai," J.D. spoke slowly and softly. Jogi's body tensed. "You got sick when you were working there."

"How do you know ... all this?" Jogi stammered.

"You possibly contracted a virus while working there."

"What virus?"

Nabeel opened his mouth to reply, but just at that moment, Saif stormed into the restaurant, panting. He mustered all of his strength and screamed:

"Turn on the TV! They caught the killer!"

. . .

A misty February fog filled the hazy air as cold, yellow sunlight slanted off the tops of minarets. Even brighter were the white marble domes of Lahore High Court, a one-hundred-and-fifty-year-old red brick building. It was majestic colonial-era architecture. Amid tall palm trees its arched windows, white stone columns, detailed wall art, and vast plaza was nothing short of a marvel, a reminder of the British-era 1800s, infused with a touch of Mughal Empire.

The world had recently witnessed the turn of the millennium. On February 8th, the hearing of Javed Iqbal had begun. A little over a month ago, he had walked into one of the local newspaper agencies and requested to be turned in.

"Hello, my name is Javed Iqbal, killer of one hundred children," he announced, as he walked up to the front desk.

The receptionist was caught off guard when an ordinary-looking man walked up to him and said that. It was shortly after nine p.m. on December 30, 1999, a busy time of night to meet deadlines, especially near the end of the year and the end of a millennium besides. The receptionist took his glasses off and looked again at the scruffy-faced man standing in front of him, searching for a slight chance that this might be a prank being played on him. With a haggard demeanor, in dirty—almost tattered—clothes, the man inquisitively gazed right into the receptionist's bloodshot, puffy eyes.

"Believe me, sir," Javed gave him a smile. "Your superiors will be very happy to hear this news. Now if you could only hurry along and tell them I am here."

The piercing glare and coldness in his eyes gave the receptionist chills. Ten minutes later, Javed Iqbal was taken into a press room, and a reporter was called in.

The city of Lahore woke up to shocking news: Javed Iqbal, the killer, had surrendered of his own will. From Ghurki to Ravi Road to Peshawar, cities, neighborhoods, and streets buzzed with the latest development. People congregated at barber shops, cafés, market squares, in front of their houses, and gossiped with great enthusiasm about what they had learned. Many wondered how something like this might have happened in their own back yard. Waiters who had served Javed food at the restaurant in Ghurki recalled the day in great detail. Neighbors could not believe they were only inches away from what appeared to be the crime of the century.

The Lahore High Court was no exception. Over-crowded with journalists, lawyers, and the friends and families of the victims, its tall, vaulted ceilings echoed with an incoherent buzzing noise. Inside the courtroom it was standing room only. It was the first day of the hearing, a busy day to cross-examine the witnesses. A crime reporter from the newspaper agency was present with a transcript of the December 30th confession, and a recording of the confession was to be played in the court. Pressed back against the closed doors amid the overpowering crowd, nearly suffocating, were Saif, Mina, and Yosef. With tired and somber looks, they gazed at the sea of people in front of them blocking the view toward the front of the court. Saif tried to jump up a couple of times to look ahead, but to no avail. They were all there to get a glimpse of the man sitting in the defendant's chair, the man accused of murdering their brothers and sons.

Finally the district judge arrived, and the proceedings began. The defense counsel and special prosecutor went to work. A tape was being played, repeatedly it seemed, but it was incomprehensible to the audience at the back of the room. Saif attempted one more time to jump up.

"I see him," he muttered upon landing back on his feet.

"You saw him?" Mina asked.

"Yes, I did."

"What is happening there?"

"Lots of talking."

"What does he look like?" Mina asked.

"Just like the photo in the newspaper, *amma*, just like that," Saif responded.

Saif spotted Nabeel standing in the crowd a few rows up. He waved at Nabeel, who caught the gesture in the corner of his eye and made his way to them.

"We should be up front," Yosef barked, as he saw Nabeel.

"It is early," Nabeel said. "Please be patient. We are doing all that we can to tame the crowd. It is a circus."

It had taken a lot of convincing by Jogi to have the gang be comfortable with Nabeel and J.D. The mention of "press" had them all scurrying in different directions. They were hesitant when Nabeel and J.D. offered to go with them to the police station and record statements. They hid when they were invited to the press office to register their grievances.

"I have nothing more to say to them." Saif had recounted his visit to the police and walked out.

Yosef simply blew cigarette smoke into J.D.'s face and had switched tables at the restaurant. It was the promise of a chance to have their voices be heard in court that had changed the gang's attitude toward the two journalists.

"It is best if we go and wait outside in the hallway," J.D. said.

Mina asked what was happening toward the front.

"They are playing the confession tape of the defendant."

"Confession tape?"

"Yes, both audio and video," Nabeel looked over his shoulder and replied.

"Did you hear it?"

"I caught it the third time."

"What did it say?" Mina asked.

Nabeel glanced at J.D. and looked away.

"You heard the tape. What did it say?" Mina grabbed J.D. by the collar of his coat.

"They heard him confess in his own voice: '*Haan khud mar dia tha sab ko*' (yes, I killed them all)."

Mina's eyes rolled back. Her body recoiled, and her head spun as she fainted. Saif grabbed her before she fell. Mina was carried out of the courtroom by Saif and Yosef.

The court session continued, playing the audio and video tapes of the confession. The defense counsel cross-examined the witness, the journalist who had interviewed Javed.

The trio came back to the courtroom on February 21 when a photo-shop owner testified that Javed had taken the photos of his victims to be developed there. Mina was able to sit and listen to the proceedings. At the insistence of the special prosecutor, the photo-shop owner was given extra time and asked to sit next to the stenographer, where he sorted through the photographs patiently.

On February 23, Constantine took the witness stand, as had others, mostly relatives of the victims. He identified six of the children in the photographs. Three of them were Raja, Daud, and Rehman.

"Drama inside court intensifies": That was the headline Superintendent Yunus read on the front page of the March 8 newspaper as he sat in his office sipping tea. The attorneys for Javed had filed a petition stating that their client was under severe mental duress and that the entire plot had been staged. They claimed that all the street children in the case were alive and challenged the court to find them.

The One Hundred

On March 16, Javed Iqbal was found guilty of one hundred murders. Staring at the defendant from his perch, the judge's voice trembled as he announced the decree.

Javed was to be hanged at the market square in front of the families of the victims, then cut into one hundred pieces and dumped in acid, as he had done with his victims.

. . .

On a bright September afternoon, the owner of Café Pyala climbed down from the roof of the café. He had just installed a brand-new antenna for better TV reception. The crowd inside the café seemed to have been drawn to the television lately. Most of its patrons rushed to get a table close to the TV as soon as they walked in. Occasional fights broke out, but were quickly resolved. Routine thumping of the TV set had made the owner curse, yell, and finally give in. They all watched intently as the case unfolded, witnesses were called, testimonies recorded. Most of all, they saw the full image of the accused.

Jogi sat in the corner across from Nabeel, J.D., and Yosef. He had just returned from the rehab center with Nabeel.

"How do you feel?" Nabeel had asked on the drive back.

At the shelter, a doctor had been called in and he had examined Jogi. He explained to Jogi what J.D. and Nabeel had already told him.

"Son, there is currently no cure for AIDS," the doctor had said.

"As good as any other day," Jogi coughed as he replied.

Nabeel had asked him about his days in Afghanistan.

Jogi told him about all the Indian and Pakistani movies he used to watch in cinemas in Afghanistan.

"I saw *'Maula Jatt'* at least ten times."

Jogi had rolled down the van's window and reminisced about Kabul as he remembered it from when he was twelve. Finding out about AIDS and hearing it from the doctor seemed to have given him some perspective and peace.

"I couldn't get over the breasts on Anjuman, the famous Pakistani actress," he laughed.

"That makes two of us. When it comes to Raquel Welch and Anjuman, Anjuman wins." They both laughed.

"Now I don't have to wonder anymore, you know," Jogi said as he inhaled deeply. "I am content."

Nabeel said nothing in response for a few minutes.

"Are you in pain?" he eventually spoke.

"Just tired," Jogi answered.

"No matter what happens, you are among friends," Nabeel said, as he kept his eyes on the road. He saw in the corner of his eye Jogi reaching out for the cigarette pack.

Jogi saw Saif walk into the cafe and motioned him over. Saif's approach was tired and slow.

"Anyone heard anything?" he asked as he sat down. "I know I have not."

Javed Iqbal's verdict had caused both domestic and international outcry from human rights commissions, the interior minister, even from religious clerics, who deemed the punishment both barbaric and a deviation from Islamic teachings.

"His lawyers are planning to appeal to the high court." Nabeel chewed on his fingernails.

"What does that mean?" Jogi asked.

J.D. explained it could delay carrying out the sentence and prolong the process.

"Anything else you want to add, Mr. Justice-for-All?" Yosef sneered.

"It certainly does not mean the battle is lost." J.D. kept his tone soft.

"But it also does not mean he has gotten what he deserves." Saif rested back in the chair.

A small crowd of urchins had gathered around them and was intently listening to the conversation.

"I told you it was useless," Yosef addressed Jogi. "Trusting these men was a mistake. Look where it got us," he sneered.

Nabeel leaned over and placed his hand on Yosef's shoulder. "Calm down, friend," he said. "Have a little faith."

"Have faith?" Yosef jerked his shoulder away. "Have faith in you, in the police? You want us to sit here and wait, to confuse us with your fancy words—" he waved a copy of the newspaper in Nabeel's face—"while the killer out there continues to elude the law."

"Javed is not going anywhere anytime soon; calm down," Nabeel snapped back.

"Can you guarantee that?" Yosef hissed. "Can you guarantee he will not con his way out of the prison?" Nabeel, flushed, stared at Yosef's face in silence.

"We live. And we die. But in the end, surviving with your head up high is what matters the most."

A heavy silence fell and drenched everyone inside, followed by the sound of the door slamming behind Yosef.

9 THE ALLIANCE

Cooco's Den was alive and bustling with regulars during the late hours of the night. The restaurant was built based on the vision of an artist whose mother and sisters were prostitutes. Nestled among some of the most historic architecture in the city, the restaurant thrived on a cobblestone street speckled with salons. It was run by courtesans and was in a red-light district of Lahore called Hira Mandi. People walking down the street could hear the muffled sounds of tabla, sitar, and anklets wafting from the rooms right above the storefronts.

Situated inside a *haveli* (private mansion) Cooco's Den stood squarely within its neighborhood's history. It was reminiscent of Indian architecture, with frescos and statues of ancient gods, goddesses, and animals. The ambience was tastefully matched with the building's history through dark wood furniture, dating as far back as the 1800s, perched in every nook and corner. Oil paintings of courtesans sprawled across red- , cinnamon- , and mustard-colored walls.

Hatim stumbled his way down the narrow, white-marble staircase after having had a late dinner on the restaurant's rooftop. The dimly lit ambience did not help his intoxicated state of mind. He had been drinking since early that evening. He took another swig of whiskey, confiscated once from a German tourist, and almost knocked down one of the paintings. No one tried to confront him. He was in his police uniform.

"Shaila!" He yelled out a name as he reached the floor. His bloodshot eyes roamed the room as he staggered to maintain balance. Concerned customers abandoned their half-eaten meals and scurried out. Hatim again called out the name of the prostitute whom he had gone to see earlier in the evening. Inside his throbbing head, as he tried to grab the back of a chair, time rolled back to the early hours of the day. There hadn't been anything unusual about the morning when he got to the police station and reported for duty. Some of the usual jokes were shared among fellow constables. One of them complained about his pregnant wife and how the cost of living would break his back. Another spread blasphemy toward the politicians. The *chai wala* (tea boy) came at his regular time and passed the tea around the room. After filing a couple of minor FIRs, Hatim had grabbed the midsection of the newspaper and sunk deeper into his chair.

He was happy to be at work and not home. His wife, Fatima, had brought him once again to one of those moods he detested: She made him think. Hatim was okay with the way things were without pondering too much about right or wrong. To him it was survival that took precedence, not moral values, ethics, or right or wrong. He was happy to provide for his family no matter what it took. He felt proud.

He had turned to look at Fatima when he had woken up in the early morning. It was time for morning *salat* (prayer), and he found her praying on the other side of the room. He watched her through sleepy eyes. Her washed face, covered by her *dupatta*, glowed under the moonlight filtering through the window. Her lips moved as she proficiently recited verses from the Quran under her breath. Her delicate features and gestures displayed utter devotion and submission to the ultimate divine power.

Not being a religious man himself, Hatim felt at peace watching his wife being a God-loving woman. He took solace in knowing that her pious spirit kept the house pure and clean. He tended to believe that her prayers, five times a day, would cover both of them on the day he might have to answer for his deeds. He smiled and felt ready to go back to sleep. Fatima saw him gazing at her as she finished *salat*. Fearful of being caught staring at her, Hatim quickly turned to other side and closed his eyes.

"I know you are awake." Fatima's voice, like a rustle of a gentle breeze, entered his ears. "You were looking at me."

"I was wondering where you went, that is all," Hatim replied with his eyes closed.

"You know very well I wake up every morning at the same time for *salat*."

"I really don't want to start an argument. If you didn't like it, then I won't look at you anymore." Hatim's back was still toward Fatima. Hatim knew all too well where this conversation was leading. They had talked about it before. And each time it had ended with Hatim smashing pots and pans against the wall.

"I want you to think about our son." Fatima kept her voice low. Hatim turned to look at her. His eyes were now wide open.

"Woman, do not start with me this early in the morning," he hissed. "I put food on the table, provide us shelter, give you clothes to wear, make sure our son goes to a good school. What else do you want from me?"

Hatim knew what Fatima was referring to. She wanted to convert him into what she called an honest-living man. She argued that food bought with money gained through bribery and extortion would burn the family's soul; that they would all be condemned in the eyes of Allah if he did not cease to work for the police. To Hatim, giving up all the perks that came with the police job meant poverty and starvation. He did not make the rules; he had justified his work over the years by believing that. He was just another pawn in this game, he used to say; who was he to refuse if someone offered him a gift—usually in the form of cash—in exchange for a minor favor?

"Yes, yes, you are providing us with everything. But you are also poisoning our souls with the money you earn through sin and corruption."

Hatim looked at her face leaning over him. He thought how beautiful she was.

"Do you really want to raise your son through *haram* (unlawful means)?"

Hatim also knew Fatima was aware of how much he loved his son, Saqib. The five-year-old's chubby cheeks had brought new light into his life. Hatim's chest swelled with pride when he walked the neighborhood with Saqib riding on his shoulder. He rushed home every day to receive a big hug from his son. Hatim loved to see Saqib's eyes brighten every time he brought his son a treat.

"What if one of the children the police pick up from the streets is one of your own?" Fatima said. She was getting better at her argument. With each talk, she hoped to invoke the God-fearing soul she hoped Hatim had, buried deep inside him. She could see in his eyes that his heart acknowledged the path to righteousness, but his mind was caught up in the materialistic, mortal glitter of the world.

"That is enough!" Hatim growled. "I don't want to hear another word about Saqib." He sprang out of bed and walked toward the washroom.

"My son is not to be compared with ordinary urchins on the street!" he said out loud, with his back toward Fatima. "What I do, how I do it, is for this family, for you, for our son!" he exclaimed, before slamming the door behind him.

Hatim felt torn each time Fatima brought up the subject. Despite his convictions to be part of the wheel, to accept donations every now and then in exchange for favors, he hadn't been able to look her in the eyes and say she was wrong. Her father was an *imam* (a religious scholar) and had seeded a deep-rooted religious teaching in all his children's hearts. Part of Hatim had become numb to those guilts over the years in the name of providing for his family. Yet the knowledge of right from wrong hadn't completely died inside him. He used to feel a little sting in his chest if the toy he bought for Saqib had come from the money he and his colleagues had collected from the street hawker selling vegetables. He smiled at Saqib when he came out wearing the brand-new clothes his father had gotten for him. Yet behind that smile, there used to be a smudge of sadness for the boy whose cart he and his friends had overturned, spilling his fruits onto the road, because he hadn't been able to make the month's allowance that the police collected from him. But that emotion had died a long time ago. The thought of Saqib being a street urchin made him cringe. Fatima exploited his emotions, and he felt angry each time she invoked the feelings he had worked so hard to suppress.

Hatim's chain of thought had broken when he heard loud noises and a commotion coming from the front room. He slammed the newspaper on the table and followed the noise. Two constables were dragging in a boy who appeared slightly over fourteen years of age. An older male wearing a suit walked behind, wiping his forehead with a handkerchief. The man introduced himself to Hatim.

"My wife's precious jewelry, he stole all of it!" the man cried to Hatim.

"How do you know it was him?" Hatim asked.

The fourteen-year-old, who had been hired as a house servant by the man, found it difficult to stand due to exhaustion. Hatim motioned the constables to let him sit on the floor. His face seemed bruised.

"We found one of her earrings tucked in his pocket when we searched him." The man waved his hands in the air. "He has stolen the jewelry and won't admit it." The man grabbed Hatim by the elbow and took him to a corner.

"We tried to make him confess, but he is a tough one," he murmured in Hatim's ear.

"I can see that," Hatim replied.

"I have spoken to your superiors. They have assured me you will take care of it." The man slid his hand inside Hatim's pocket, dropping a bundle of cash. Hatim could tell the currency was crisp.

"I just want my wife to be happy again. She is devastated by the loss of her precious jewelry."

Hatim motioned the constables to take the boy into another room.

"We'll do all we can to recover your belongings, sir."

"I am happy to hear that." The profusely sweating man in the suit smiled.

Happy to see their share waiting in Hatim's pocket, the other constables grabbed the boy and dragged him away.

A stifling sun had perched high up in the sky, making even the coolest of shadows cry for clemency. Hatim turned the black swivel table fan to high speed and stood close to it, feeling the warm breeze slapping against his face. He should be in the room with the other constables like many other times in the past, he thought. Many in his field of work had given him credit for making criminals confess. His creative techniques, which had the strongest of them speaking within hours, were lauded by his peers. He should be in there, he thought, making the boy speak quickly without too much effort on his part. The boy looked feeble. He didn't stand a chance of prolonged interrogation.

Yet he could feel his heart beating fast, sweat running down his cheekbones in that humidity-soaked air. Hatim tried to fight the feeling. He tried to muster his strength and complete the job. He hated the fact that his wife's nagging had made him feel torn between values of morality. He should've been inside the room slapping the kid around till he confessed. But instead, he was outside contemplating.

He heard a scream come from the other room.

This will be taken as a sign of weakness by my peers, he thought. The hesitance will throw me out of the circle. The pack I have worked so hard to be part of will disown me.

Another scream filled the air.

"What if your own son was one of the street urchins?" Fatima's voice echoed in his head. He saw her pure, fresh, silky face leaning over his. "Do the right thing, Hatim," he heard her say. "Allah almighty is watching. Don't let your sins darken the hearts of your family." He saw her praying: prostrate, with both hands joined together and palms facing up. She was praying God would wash away his sins. She was his savior.

The next scream was louder than the last one.

Hatim dashed over and slammed the door open. The teen was sitting on a chair, his hands tied to the back of it, his head cocked to the side, his eyes barely open. The air smelled of burnt skin. One of the constables had extinguished his cigarette against the teen's left temple. Hatim grabbed the boy's head between his hands.

"You do not want to test my patience, not today!" he growled, his face turning red. "Speak now and speak fast, boy." One of the constables splashed cold water on the boy's face.

"Tell me where you hid the jewelry, and I will go easy on you," Hatim said to him, as he saw the boy's eyes fully open.

"I swear to you, *sahib*. I did not steal anything." The boy's voice was weak. Hatim could detect he had an accent. He wasn't a local. It was common practice for teenage boys to come to Lahore from small villages in other provinces to earn wages, or in some instances be brought in by their parents.

"I can tell you are not from here," Hatim said, staring in his eyes. "And I can sense you have never been in police custody before. You don't know how we operate. I am giving you this one last chance to come clean and be honest with me before I start ripping your fingernails from your skin, one by one." Hatim felt his left hand shaking with the rising temper inside him.

Several shades of fear crawled over the boy's face. Hatim grabbed the boy's chin in his other hand and leaned closer to him.

"I am not a thief. Please let me go," the boy pleaded, in a barely audible voice.

Hatim felt his coworkers standing in the back, watching his shaky hand and grinning. He sensed one of them covered his mouth and whispered something to the other. He could swear he saw Fatima's shadow standing in the corner, asking him to have mercy. Hatim let go of boy's face and straightened up.

The boy opened his mouth to speak, sensing his plea might have taken effect. He noticed the facial expression on Hatim's face softening. The boy's heart, for a brief moment, tried to beat normally. But before any words left his mouth, Hatim's fist struck his jaw, knocking him and the chair to which he was tied to the floor. A pool of thick, red blood oozed from his face and painted the gray cement floor.

"*Haramzade*! (born out of wedlock)" Hatim bellowed. "You will be sorry you did not take the chance I gave you and be honest with me."

For the next fifteen minutes, the boy remained on the floor, his hands still tied to the back of the chair. Hatim and the other two constables kicked and punched him even after his body stopped moving ten minutes into the beating.

. . .

Hatim raised his head; someone was shaking his shoulder. Through blurry vision he saw a shop owner with a concerned look on his face. Hatim grabbed his constantly spinning head. An empty bottle of whiskey lay sideways on the table in front of him. Cooco's Den was almost empty. He stumbled his way out of the restaurant into the deserted street. Light from the lamp posts had dimmed, and the cobbled street was bathed in the blue light of the pre-dawn hour. His steps small, his shoulders down, he walked toward the shimmering rays of the rising sun, which was fighting off the blue darkness. Fatima must be done with morning prayers and would now be making her breakfast of freshly baked flat bread, tea, and eggs. He suddenly felt hungry. But what was he going to tell her about where he had spent the night? How could he tell her that at about the same time she was praying for his safety, he was cupping a prostitute's breasts, ripping her clothes off, his alcohol-soaked breath steaming up her neck? He straightened up his posture and turned the corner. A shadow followed him a few feet away.

And what would he say to her about beating the boy nearly to death with his colleagues at the station? He contemplated whether he should mention that he had seen her silhouette in the room. Hatim felt emotionally captive as he walked faster and faster down the streets. Fatima never asked him for an explanation. She never frowned over his misgivings. Yet he felt compelled to answer to her. He knew all too well that, without her, he would fall apart. She was his pillar. "Fatima." He exhaled her name with each breath passing through his lips. He wanted to put his head into her lap and weep, hoping her pure and pious persona would shelter him from his demons.

His steps were no longer staggering. There was a sense of resolution in his eyes. He wanted to get home as quickly as possible. He was outside Hira Mandi. Fruit and vegetable hawkers were loading up their carts with fresh produce. Butchers were busy hanging freshly slaughtered beef at their storefronts. On the far end, a milkman loaded vats of unpasteurized milk for home delivery. A group of cackling children in uniforms crossed the street on their way to school. A new day had arrived. Hatim walked past a series of shops on the street with glass storefronts. His gaze shifted for a brief moment to one of the glass walls on the right before he turned sharply and faced the shadow that had been following him for a while.

Yosef froze in his tracks when he saw Hatim turn and face him. Hatim's eyes bored into Yosef's face before he shifted his gaze to the bundle of cash clutched in Yosef's hand.

"Who are you, and why are you following me?" Hatim grunted, his eyes fixed on the stack of cash.

"I have a proposition you might be interested in," Yosef swallowed saliva down his dry throat and uttered.

. . .

Two boys walked through *Gora Kabristan*, the only Christian cemetery in the city, amid worn-out tombs and dried flowers. Weeds and wild tallgrass had grown on the outer edge of the graveyard. The dog Rambo followed right behind them. The air smelled of incense, roses, and freshly watered earth. An eerie silence of death around them resonated with the fast-approaching fall chill.

"You did fucking what?" Jogi barked.

Yosef thought about Hatim's damp, reddened eyes piercing through him. Hatim had staggered a bit as he tightened his grip on Yosef's arms. And then he had taken another look at the cash in Yosef's hand.

"And why would I waste my time listening to someone like you?" Hatim had said, leaning over Yosef. He could smell fear dripping from the boy's face. Backlight from the rising sun created a halo around Hatim's head.

"You would have strangled me to death and taken the money by now if you weren't the least bit interested in what I had to say." Yosef had inhaled Hatim's sweat-soaked body odor. "Yet you and I are still talking."

"And you don't think I might still break your neck and walk away with my pockets stuffed with cash?" Hatim snickered.

"You had the opportunity to get rid of me once, but you didn't," Yosef answered.

Hatim's eyes squinted as he searched the back of his mind to see if he recognized the boy standing in front of him.

"I remember you," Hatim said, as bleak signs of recognition entered into his eyes. "Yes, it is coming to me now." He grabbed Yosef's face between his thumb and index finger and turned it sideways.

"I see all your wounds have healed nicely," he said.

"Not all of them."

Hatim stared at his face for a while, as if trying to read it.

"You are just as much of a loudmouth as I remember. And you are following me around, even after what I did to your face back then?"

"And you may very well do it again," Yosef answered, "but at least you will let me walk away if you don't like what I have to say."

"I cannot wait to hear what you have to say," Hatim said with a slithery smirk on his face.

Hatim grabbed Yosef by the collar and dragged him into a nearby restaurant.

"Leave the money on the table," he told Yosef.

He sat across the table and listened while Yosef talked. His body language changed several times during that talk: frowns appeared on his forehead, quickly replaced by an arched right eyebrow. His eyes widened in amazement as he perched his chin between his thumb and index finger, followed by a laugh. He extended his legs outwards and placed his hands behind his head, assuming a more relaxed position.

Yosef continued to talk, uninterrupted. Both his hands were placed on the table, shaking, palms facing down.

Toward the end, Hatim leaned over and said, "I don't believe in coincidences, but this is fucking amazing."

Yosef's face turned pale. He slowly slid farther into the back of the chair.

"On any other day, I would have twisted your neck and left you here to rot." Hatim thought about the night he had spent and his conversation with Fatima. "But today is your lucky day!"

"It needed to be done," Yosef answered Jogi and sauntered through the graveyard with his head down, tossing tiny rocks aside with his feet.

"Where did you get the money from?" Jogi asked.

"It doesn't matter where it came from," Yosef replied. Aside from Daud, no one knew that the money had come with him from Mingora. "What's important is what it will be used for."

They walked out of the cemetery and turned east. A few yards down, two figures emerged around a street corner. The man was wearing plain clothes and a *pakol* beaded with glass seeds. His companion, a female, stood covered in a gray shawl from her head down to her knees. Her large, shimmering eyes above her covered nose and mouth gazed at Yosef.

"Neelam." The name breathed out from his mouth like blue smoke, mixed in with the steam of his breath. He stopped in his tracks. The man walked over and whispered something in Yosef's ears. Yosef asked Jogi if he could join his friend later.

"Yosef, don't …" Jogi touched him on the elbow.

"I'll be okay, I promise," Yosef smiled. He wondered if they could hear the drumming of his heart pounding through his chest.

The man, who was Neelam's house servant, sat on a bench as Yosef and Neelam stood under a tree in the nearby park. Her eyes ran over his face, pained at the sight of the scars that hadn't been there the last time they were together. Tiny little stars sparkled in her eyes, as tears filled them and spilled onto her cheeks.

"I did not expect to see you again." Yosef's voice was broken, his words wounded.

"I am sorry, Yosef." Her lower lip quivered as she bit into it. "Can you forgive me?"

"There is nothing to forgive," Yosef answered.

"My mother threatened to drink poison if I did not lead my father to you," Neelam tried to explain, soaked in guilt. Yosef asked her to stop talking.

"The look on your face that day told me what you must have gone through."

Neelam placed her head on Yosef's chest.

"I have left everything behind if you will take me," she said softly. "We can take the bus to another city. Are you with me, Yosef?"

Yosef tilted her face up by holding her chin. He looked into her sublime eyes and felt the softness of her skin, washed in milk and rose petals.

"Nothing would soothe my soul more than being with you," he said. "The memories of the time we spent together blanket me during cold and lonely nights." Yosef took a few steps back. "But to drag you with me into the hell of uncertainty would be the biggest sin I commit if we ran off."

Neelam pleaded with him to reconsider, asking him to imagine the beginning of a new life together.

"I am sorry, Neelam. I am a street urchin. You are the *noor* of a noble family." Yosef thought of Hatim counting the money at the restaurant.

"It is not in my *kismet* (luck) to be loved by someone like you." His mind raced toward the deal he had made with the devil.

He watched Neelam, shatter-hearted, disappear at the turn of the corner. Only then did he allow the tears welling in his eyes to gush down his face. He called her name as he cupped his face and wept.

. . .

The sky turned from bright blue to dark grey in a matter of minutes as they watched through dusty, high glass windows inside an abandoned warehouse. The first drop of rain splattered on the glass right where Saif's nose was pressed against it. He watched the thunderous clouds intently rolling in, getting ready to drench the city. The mood inside the room was just as dark and gloomy. They all perched on furniture made up of bottle crates, truck tires, and an old construction dolly.

"I don't understand the point of this."

Nabeel broke the silence. He had chosen to lean against a pillar. He had cursed under his breath when he had agreed to meet Yosef. He had driven like a madman through the congested midday traffic after hearing Yosef's voice. Upon arrival, Nabeel's jaw dropped when he was told about the plan being brewed. Now he wished he had not come to this meeting.

"I am hoping one of you will burst into laughter and tell me it is all a big joke." No one replied.

The room lit up, followed by a thunderous sound. The sound of pounding rain right above their heads intensified.

"Are you in, or are you out?" Jogi asked.

Nabeel gave them a scornful look.

"What makes you think you will get away with this?"

"Leave that to us," Yosef said. His head was down when he spoke. He bounced a tennis ball off the floor.

What was being proposed was beyond absurd. He had never heard anything like this. Not only was it criminal; it was almost impossible.

"What if I inform the police?"

"You turn me in, there will be someone waiting to take my place," Yosef said. "That is not a concern."

Nabeel looked around at the group of youngsters and teenagers in front of him. Their eyes were resolute, their will unquestionable, their task ... unimaginable.

"You can't possibly expect me to be a part of this." Nabeel's face had turned red.

"I told you not to get him involved," Jogi said, sitting in a dark corner, barely visible. "It doesn't make much news for him to sell. That is why he is not interested."

"That is not true," Nabeel protested. "Look, I understand how you all must be feeling. I realize the pain and agony …."

"He has been transferred back to jail, yeah?" Yosef asked.

Nabeel looked at him helplessly.

"Yes or no?"

"Yes," Nabeel said diffidently. "His sentence as announced cannot be carried out due to pressure from human rights commissions."

"How long before a final verdict might be announced?"

"It could take … years," Nabeel admitted.

"Is it still possible that his sentence might be reduced?" Yosef asked.

Nabeel replied with silence.

Yosef moved closer to Nabeel. "Did you ever feel there was a monster living, walking, breathing among you, all around you, swallowing its prey patiently, one at a time, and there was no one you could turn to for help?"

Nabeel's hand reached for the tiny beads of sweat protruding on his forehead. Yet he could not tear his gaze away from Yosef's expressionless, icy face.

"Do you see how helplessness teaches survival in its own way to those who are on their own? Can you understand why we must finish what the law has failed to accomplish?"

"Justice may still prevail." Nabeel spoke in a choking voice. He felt the hollowness of his own words. There was no weight, no conviction, no resolution in what he had said. How could he possibly expect these street children to believe a statement he himself would mock if told? These children were well aware of harsh reality; they lived in it day and night. He felt cornered. With so many eyes fixated on him, he found it difficult to breathe. Aside from the furious beating of his own heart, the only other sound Nabeel heard was the sound of the words coming out of Yosef's mouth:

"Javed Iqbal must die!"

10 BREAK-IN

October 10, 2000

The clock tower at the railway station, with an architecture reminiscent of the British imperial era, chimed in the still of the night. It was midnight. The last train had arrived; the passengers had deboarded, and now were united with the ones who had been awaiting their arrival. *Qulees* (porters) rushed the luggage off the train and thanked passengers who tipped them. A lone, late-night street vendor selling grilled kebabs put a tarp over his cart and called it a night, leaving behind the occasional distant puttering sound of rickshaws and barking dogs.

Jogi took another puff from the cigarette. The red amber of burning tobacco shimmered in the black night.

"You awake?" he asked Saif. Blue smoke hovered around his face.

"Yes."

"Then say something." Jogi turned to look at him.

"I just did. What do you want?" Saif replied.

"Are you alert?"

"Yes."

"Scared?"

"No."

"Say it if you are." Saif did not respond. Far up on a tree, an owl hooted. Saif could hear the sound of burning paper as Jogi took another deep, hard puff from the cigarette. He looked up. The sky was clear after days of rain. Countless stars speckled across it like infinite sparkling dots.

"I am afraid what tomorrow might bring," Saif said.

"You are afraid of what you don't know."

"Aren't we all?" Saif asked.

"So you are scared."

"A little."

Jogi followed Saif's gaze and looked at the sky.

"The sun will rise again, the stars will disappear for one more night. We may feel less afraid and more free by the end of this night. I don't see much changing tomorrow."

"I have never done this before. What if something does go wrong?" Saif shifted his eyes toward Jogi.

He had been feeling a little weak in his resolve lately. A few days ago when Yosef and Jogi had talked to him, all he could think about was his little brother. The image of Raja's face ran over and over in his head, all the time they had spent together both bonding and fighting. He realized that each moment spent with him, good or bad, had brought the two closer. And then Raja had disappeared from under his watch, never to come back. For so long he had blamed himself for Raja's disappearance. The tormented thought of how he could have done things differently the day Raja vanished kept him awake at nights. And his heart had filled with rage when Yosef said that the man responsible for Raja's death might roam free soon.

"Word on the street is that he has he gotten himself out of situations like this?" Yosef's voice echoed in Saif's head. "What makes this time any different than others if it is true? He will be out again, and you will look over your shoulder with every breath you take. If he can bribe the police to get out of jail in the past, he can again fill their pockets to have them look the other way when he is hunting us down on the streets and bazaars and market squares."

Saif thought about his mother, who had gone quiet. There were no questions left. Her searching eyes, previously flickering with fading hope, had gone dark and still. Saif had watched her as she made a plate of food for his dinner the other night. She sat across from him, silent, stirring the pot aimlessly. She only answered if spoken to. Saif wondered if deep down she detested him for losing her youngest son. He wondered why she didn't grab him by the collar and slap him till she dropped from exhaustion. She ran her hand over his head and kissed his forehead instead, each time he left the house after dinner.

But he felt torn and doubtful sitting next to Jogi on the night for which all was planned. He hated the sickening feeling in his stomach. Jogi grabbed his trembling hands and squeezed them.

"Do you remember the time last year, right at this train station, when we had a fight?" Jogi asked.

"I do."

"How that *qulee* tried to cheat me out of my wage after I helped him unload the luggage?"

"And what we did to him in the end," Saif chuckled.

"You pulled his drawstring, causing his pants to drop on the crowded platform." Jogi smiled. They both laughed.

"I remember," Saif said. Jogi offered him a cigarette.

"Do you get my point?"

"I get it," Saif replied, after a hesitant pause.

Jogi looked ahead into the darkness, his eyes squinted and focused. A drifting patch of cloud covered the moonlight, making the night even darker. In the distance, a shadow slipped through the blackness and moved toward them. Under the lamp post, it shaped into Yosef, approaching gingerly.

"The fact that you are with us tonight makes me want to believe you want the same thing. You heard what everyone said, how they scolded us, asking us to let go. But you don't want to let go of your brother's death and the way he died. That is why you are here. Those who came to our help initially later bailed, saying justice would prevail. The law is not on the street urchins' side, and you know it. You can swallow your anger and call it misfortune. Or you can be with us tonight and bring closure to what's been eating you from inside." Jogi paused as he waved to Yosef.

"You are courageous." Jogi tuned to look at Saif. "But brave ones get afraid, too. Fear of the unknown is always scary. Yosef is coming." Jogi nodded with his chin toward a now swiftly approaching Yosef. "This is your chance to leave, to walk away. If you leave tonight, no one will point a finger at you in the morning. But tomorrow and every day after that, you and only you will have to live with the clouds of guilt and doubts. It is your call, my friend."

"I want to stay," Saif said.

"Then be strong and make us strong. Your weakness can take us down." Jogi patted Saif's shoulder. Yosef emerged from the dark, a little breathless.

"It is time. You all ready?" he asked.

. . .

On the mountain's slope,

The assembled trees form a dark green mass.

The stars twinkle,

And the moonlight adorns the Valley.

It is a night of youth and love.

From the grassy meads, covered with wild flowers,

Where the nightingales sing,

I hear the heavenly melody of the shepherd's flute.

Jogi's harmonious humming resonated as they walked the empty roads, amid the rolled shutters of closed storefronts.

"What is that you sing, friend, and in what language?" Yosef asked.

Jogi told him about the folksong that his father used to sing at dusk in Pushto, his native language; it was one of the few faded memories of home remaining in his mind.

"Every evening, during our walk back home after closing the shop at sunset, father hummed this song. It always seemed to make the trip home at the end of the day shorter," Jogi said. "Tonight reminded me of the dusty gravel road we walked, him starting with a whistle and then carrying the tune, trying to match the high pitch of chirping birds on the trees."

"It sounds beautiful."

"Thanks, *bhai*," Jogi replied.

"You miss your family?"

Jogi thought about the day he had boarded the bus, leaving Afghanistan for Pakistan.

"Every hour of every day."

They turned the corner and walked in silence. Jogi's humming faded into the darkness, and his breath became uneven.

"We should slow down," Saif said.

"What gave you that idea?"

"You don't look so good."

"I am fine. Besides, there is no time." Jogi brushed off the suggestion. "Let's continue," he offered with a weak smile, and lit a cigarette. He tried to hide it, but it was apparent to both Saif and Yosef that he was losing his strength.

"Have you been taking the pills?" Saif asked.

"Yes."

"Don't seem to be doing much good."

"It gets me through the day."

"You need to get better."

"It is as good as it will ever get," Jogi responded. They finally turned the corner onto the street that led directly to the police station.

"What do you mean by that?" Yosef asked.

"One more time, your source is reliable, yes?" Jogi changed the subject and asked.

"Yes, yes, very reliable," Yosef replied. "You're having doubts?"

"Not for a second. I want to make sure we come out the same way we go in."

"Hatim is waiting for us at the police station. His job is to let us slip in and show us the cell Javed is kept in. We go inside, do the job, and get out."

"And you are sure Hatim will come through?"

"His pockets are filled with the money I gave him. He doesn't care. Besides, he hates Javed's guts just as much as we do."

"What about the security guard, the other constables?" Saif asked.

"We will have a window of one hour during which they will all be sent away by Hatim," Yosef answered.

"I admire your confidence."

"I am with friends I trust. I am confident," Yosef said.

The yellow-brick building became visible at the next turn of the road. The sight gave Jogi a renewed sense of energy. They started walking faster.

"You did not my answer my question," Yosef said, as he caught up with Jogi.

"I was hoping it would drop from your mind."

"I want to make sure you will be okay."

"I wish I could give you that assurance, my friend."

"Is it serious?"

"Yes."

"What is it?"

Jogi remembered sitting in front of the doctor, who had flipped the pages of Jogi's test report. Jogi did not understand the words used, such as "CD4," "viral load," "stage 4 of the disease." He remembered the concerned look in the doctor's eyes when he spoke with Constantine, Nabeel, and J.D.

"There is no cure for what you have, son," he had heard the doctor say. "There is no cure for AIDS."

"They told me to continue to take the pills, till the time comes."

Heavy silence fell around them.

"Can't the shelter give you more pills to make it better?" Yosef felt a pinch in his heart.

"The medicine is to make my remaining time here peaceful, not to prolong it. They said it is too late. Besides, more powerful pills are too expensive for them to give to me," Jogi replied with a weak smile. "I guess I won't live to grow as old as you."

"Jogi, I am so sorry to hear—"

Something hit Yosef hard on his right jaw before he could finish the sentence. As if struck by a train, his feet left the ground. He flew a few feet in the air before falling flat onto the ground. His ear ringing, numbness ran through his body followed by shooting pain. He looked up while struggling to rise. He saw four tall figures standing in front of him. One of them had twisted Jogi's arm behind his back; another had pinned Saif to the ground. One man hobbled up to Yosef and pulled him up by grabbing his hair. His teeth clenched, Yosef looked right into man's eyes. Akbar was staring right at him.

"Did you think you could hide from me forever, you *harami*?" Akbar slapped Yosef on the face, landing him back on the ground. Yosef tried to crawl away from Akbar.

"Get up and face me. I want to see how strong you are now," Akbar bellowed, as he dragged Yosef back toward him by clawing onto his ankle.

"Be careful, my friend." Hatim emerged in the dark from behind a tree. "I do not want a dead street urchin in my hands."

"Not to worry. I won't let him die that easily," Akbar hissed. "With your permission, I will take him back to Mingora, the village he ran from. He owes me quite a debt."

"What you do outside my district is your business," Hatim responded nonchalantly, while chewing tobacco.

Akbar jerked Yosef back onto his feet.

"I am going to break your legs just like you broke mine." Akbar's lips touched Yosef's ear as he whispered the words. "The crippled you will then work for me for the rest of your life."

Yosef, staggering to keep his balance and barely conscious, looked up at Hatim.

"We had a deal."

"Ah yes, the deal." Hatim paced slowly, circling around Yosef. "Once Akbar told me that the money you gave me you had stolen from him and offered to double the prize if I led him to you, I felt justified to break our little promise." A smirk crawled all over his face.

"Let's face it, *bacha*. You are a scumbag, an eating-out-of-a-garbage-can cockroach. I, on the other hand, tend to think of myself as a business man. I go with the better offer and deal."

A stream of tears rolled down from Yosef's eyes.

"Did you think I was that stupid to let a bunch of street urchins walk into my station and kill a prisoner?" Hatim grabbed Yosef by the chin.

"That prisoner is a child killer and you know it," Yosef sneered.

"You are a fucking nobody! It is not your job to pass judgment on what happens to him."

"How much will it cost for you to let him walk free?" Yosef spat on the ground. Hatim's eyes widened in amazement for a moment before the smile returned on his face.

"You know, *bacha*, you are brave. I am impressed by your courage, I must admit. But you are also an idiot. You think you can play these games and walk all over the rules made to run the society. We rule this city. We are the law. You don't get to say who goes in or walks out of my precinct."

"Take him out of my sight," Hatim said to Akbar, and turned away.

The man holding Jogi suddenly dropped to the ground, followed by the bone-shattering sound of a metal pipe striking his skull. Hatim froze in his steps. Meera and his gang emerged into the light and tackled the man holding Saif.

"What the fuck do you think you are doing?" Hatim growled. "Do you know who I am?"

"I know all about you, *sahib*, and what you do to urchins living on the street. I want to see how strong you are tonight without the uniform," Meera responded.

Akbar hobbled away from Yosef, but was met by a punch in the face from Jogi, a punch that threw him to the ground. Jogi leaned over to Yosef and held him in his arms.

"It will be okay, my friend. It will be," he said.

"You thought it through, didn't you?" Yosef grabbed him by the shoulders. A small pool of blood spilled from the corner of his mouth.

"I wanted to make sure you succeeded. That is why I asked Meera's group to follow us right behind and intervene if something went wrong."

"You must hurry. We don't have much time. The guards and constables will be back within the hour," Yosef spoke through broken breaths.

"How do we enter the police station without Hatim?" Jogi asked. They turned to look. Hatim had disappeared. Yosef rolled his eyes and dropped unconscious.

Hatim ran as fast as he could toward the police station. He had quickly realized he was outnumbered. He tiptoed away from Meera and his gang, who were busy kicking and punching Akbar and his men, and dashed off. Panting and sweating profusely, he cursed under his breath for deciding not to bring his revolver with him and instead leave it at the police station. He did not think there would be a need for a gun to tackle a bunch of street urchins and had thought that Akbar's men would take care of everything. The police station was empty when he slammed the doors open and entered. He had sent the constables on duty on nightly rounds. The idea of collecting extortion from Akbar and not sharing with the rest had enticed him quite a bit. They weren't likely to come back before completing their rounds. He frantically reached for the edge of the desk where he had left his revolver. It wasn't there. He jerked open the drawers and shuffled through the stacks of papers before realizing his gun was missing.

"Looking for this?" The voice startled Hatim. He looked up and saw Saif pointing the gun at him.

"This is not a toy, *bacha*." Hatim's voice was slightly above a whisper, his gaze locked on Saif's face. "Hand the gun over to me, and I will let you walk away."

"What cell is Javed held in?" Saif asked.

"You really don't want me to hurt you now, do you, *bacha*?" Hatim raised his hands forward and inched toward Saif.

"Answer the question and stay where you are!" Saif yelled. His grip tightened.

"My constables should be on their way back. They will be here any minute. They will shoot you if they see you pointing this gun at me."

"No they won't," Jogi entered the room. "I saw them stuffing their stomachs at Hira Mandi. I am sure they would be pleased to visit some of the courtesans to make the night more pleasurable. No, they are not coming back soon." Jogi took the gun from Saif.

"Safety was on," he said, as he unlocked the revolver and pointed it at Hatim.

"Get down on your knees," Jogi said, his voice calm and his face robbed of any expression.

"Jogi, *bacha*, you and I have been friends." Hatim's tone turned polite as he reminded Jogi of the times he had provided protection for his gang.

"You are not my friend," Jogi sneered. "You needed a pawn on the street to collect *batha* (bribes). You will never be my friend. Now do as I say before I shoot your legs one at a time."

Hatim's knees slowly moved to the floor, his hands remaining forward as a gesture of surrender.

"You will regret this." Hatim's teeth clenched.

"You are talking to someone who has nothing left to lose. That should make you very afraid," Jogi responded.

Beads of sweat appeared on Hatim's face.

"You made a promise to Yosef. I want you to keep that promise. Give me the keys to the Javed's cell, and I will make sure doctors will be able to take the bullet out of your body. I promise I will let you live."

"You kill me and the entire police force will hunt you like mad dogs into every corner of the city."

"Perhaps you didn't hear me. I don't care what happens to me in the morning. They can line me up and shoot me with a firing squad. It won't make a difference."

"I can make you very happy if you put the gun down," Hatim tried to bargain. "You can have the money I got from your friend and also from Akbar. Take the money and leave the city. I promise no one will come after you."

"You are wasting valuable time. I will find the way to the cell either way after I kill you. Put your hands behind your head and say your final prayers." Jogi pressed the hammer with the sound of a click.

The color drained from Hatim's face. The faces of his wife and child ran in front of him. He wondered if it was too late to ask God for forgiveness. His greed had taken over what could have been a turning point in his life to make amends for all the wrongs he had done in his past. He looked into Jogi's eyes past the muzzle of the revolver. They were stone cold. He could read on Jogi's marble-white face that he was ready to pull the trigger.

"Wait!" he shouted "Third cell on the right past the hallway. The key is in the middle drawer."

Jogi motioned Saif to take out the key. "You just saved your wife from being a widow," he said, and hit Hatim on the head with the handle of the revolver, knocking him unconscious.

The 6x8 cell had yellow-painted walls, a cold concrete floor, and a narrow, hard wooden bench attached to the wall on which Javed lay flat. His fingers ran over writing carved on the wall, his eyes staring at the ceiling, when he heard footsteps approaching the cell. He sprang up and stared into the hallway.

"I must have visitors," he murmured, holding the iron bars. Jogi and Saif saw Javed staring right at them.

"My children have come for a visit at an odd hour, but pleasant nonetheless." His teeth became visible through parted lips. Saif looked through the cell bars at the man. It reminded him of climbing up the wall and staring through the barred transom at Raja's clothes and bracelet. A thousand ants crawled inside his skin, thinking about this man behind the bars killing his brother and dismembering his body.

"Are you with me, brother?" Jogi placed his hand on Saif's shoulder and squeezed.

"Open the door, and let me in," Saif said.

Javed's expression changed as he saw Jogi turning the key and motioning Saif to enter through the open gate.

"Hello, children. How nice of you to come visit this old man," he said.

Saif stared into Javed's eyes and didn't say anything.

"I would ask how you managed to get inside the cell, but that would ruin the pleasant surprise."

"Do you remember a boy named Raja?" Saif asked.

"Raja, hmm ... ." Javed stared into space as if trying to recall. "I had so many friends, it is hard to remember, you know,"

"He was my brother." Saif's voice was trembling.

"Raja, Raja … oh yes, the sweet little boy just like you."

"You hired him for day labor at the market square."

"Yes, yes. He talked about you. He admired how you took care of him," Javed responded, his eyes widening.

"Did you kill him?"

"What?"

"Did you kill my brother?"

"*Bacha*, you should not believe everything you see on TV."

"I saw his clothes and bracelet on the floor in your house!" Saif yelled. "He went into your house and never came back."

"You, your brother, and your friend standing behind you, you are all the same, ungrateful bastards!" Javed shook his head. "You think you are the victim. You don't have the slightest clue what it is like to be a victim."

"I want to hear you say it."

"Say what?"

"That you killed my brother."

"Will that put you at ease?"

"No, it will make squeezing the last breath out of your body all the more satisfactory," Jogi responded instead.

"Your brother was the last of those who came before him. I helped set him free. He had already suffered enough. I helped him."

"You took someone from me who did not belong to you." Saif's eyes were bloodshot. Jogi thought about Saif's mood a little while ago, scared and confused. Now he was engulfed in rage.

"No, not me. This society took him away from you. I was just a medium. These people who breathe among you, they failed you, your brother, and ninety-nine others just like you."

From afar, the sound of *azaan* echoed in a captivating, melodic tune. It was almost dawn. Jogi felt tense. They had to leave pretty soon before the constables returned from the night shift and the morning shift staff arrived. His lips parted to let Saif know of the critical time crunch, but words would not come out. He retracted his arm, raised to grab Saif by the shoulder. Saif deserved the time he needed to face his brother's killer. He needed closure, Jogi thought.

"He called for you."

"What?"

"Raja kept looking at the door till his last breath, hoping you would return." Javed rested the back of his head on the wall.

Saif took one step back.

"You murderer!" Saif bellowed.

Javed's eyes were bright and carried the excitement of telling a tale.

"He thought you would come and save him." Javed stared into space. "But you didn't come."

One more step backward, and his back hit the iron bars of the cell gate.

"But here you are in the wee hours of the morning, looking for revenge," Javed continued.

His back pressed against the bars, Saif slid to the floor. He cupped his face.

"But can you avenge your brother?"

Saif started sobbing.

"You are a coward, weak," Javed sneered, "crying like a girl."

There was no response, only the sound of Saif weeping.

"You don't have it in you to take someone's life. I pity you. Now wipe those tears and get out of here with your friend before I shout for help."

"He is not the only one who lost his brother." A sound emerged from the hallway. Yosef, wounded and battered, staggered into the cell.

"Amazing! There are more and more—" Javed could not finish the sentence. Jogi's punch to his face landed him on the floor.

"And I am not here to get your confession. I know what you have done," Yosef said. Without wasting any time, he snatched the sheet from the bench. "Make sure he does not scream," he said to Jogi. He rolled the sheet into a rope and coiled it around Javed's neck from behind.

"You killed someone very dear to me. Now it is time for you to die." Javed's hands fluttered to grab Yosef, but to no avail.

"You either stay where you are or leave the cell, now." Yosef looked at Saif who was wiping tears from his cheeks and had a bewildered look on his face. Without wasting any more time, Yosef hands tightened around the rope, strangling Javed, squeezing his neck. Yosef's body shook and the veins in his neck and arms popped, applying all the power he could muster. Javed's eyeballs got bigger and bigger. His legs shook violently as he tried to free himself. His gaze met that of Saif, sitting right across from him, before he raised his head to face Yosef, inches above him.

"Time for you to die, motherfucker," Yosef said, staring down at him, and gave one last squeeze. Javed took one heavy breath from his mouth, his fingers fluttered for a few seconds, and his legs jerked a couple more times. And then he became motionless, his body turning limp. Jogi took his hand off Javed's body and looked at Yosef. Drops of sweat dripped down Yosef's face, and he continued to apply pressure to Javed's neck. A minute later, Jogi grabbed his arm.

"You can let go, my friend. He is dead. Javed Iqbal is dead."

11 GOODBYE

January 19, 2001

A small convoy, obviously a funeral procession, walked toward the *kabristan*. Members of the convoy took turns carrying an open-faced, wooden bedstead. A corpse, shrouded in an unstitched cotton sheet, lay on the bed as the convoy offered shoulders and shared the burden till they reached its final destination. The convoy walked through the streets past the gathered crowd which, with puzzled eyes and with hands covering mouths, whispered and wondered who had died.

The air felt dense and smoky. The sunlight filtering through the leaves was crisp. Another spring had arrived. Their nostrils filled with the fragrance of fresh roses and marigolds sewn into necklaces, being sold by street vendors. The aromatic smoke of incense hovered around them as they entered the cemetery gate. Nabeel stood few feet away, waiting. Saif saw him and waved.

"Is he here?" Saif asked as he got closer.

"Yes, I brought him with me," Nabeel answered. "He is waiting for you behind the willow tree."

Saif stomped over dried tall grass toward the tree where Yosef stood. Time had helped heal the wounds, but the scars were still visible. Dried, black scabs had replaced open cuts and wounds on his face. His left hand was in a bandage, and he hobbled a bit as he took one step forward. He smiled as he saw Saif approaching.

The last time Saif had seen Yosef was three months ago on the night he thought would never end. He vividly remembered screaming frantically, watching Javed's leg fluttering inches from him while he took his last breath. Yosef's voice came to him as if coming from under water. He was shaking Saif's shoulder, asking him to calm down, which he followed with a slap on the cheek.

"Stop shouting," Yosef's voice echoed in his ear. "It is over. Lets go!"

Jogi and Yosef had hurried him up on his feet and rushed out of the jail cell, leaving Javed's motionless body behind. Their fleeing feet came to a stop when they saw Hatim sitting on his chair, elbows resting on his knees, head cupped in his hands. Jogi took calculated steps and put the gun on the table. Hatim did not raise his head, but they heard him say as they walked out the door:

"Don't let me see your faces again."

Outside, Nabeel had been waiting for them in his jeep, engine running.

"Get in!" he shouted. Jogi helped Yosef roll onto the back seat and hopped onto the front seat with Saif. Tires spat pebbles and dirt as they screeched on the gravel road. The jeep took off at full throttle.

"How is he?" Nabeel asked Jogi.

"Injured," Jogi replied.

"He killed him." Saif said in a shaking voice. "Yosef killed Javed."

Nabeel turned to look at Jogi. His lips didn't part, but a question lingered in his eyes. Jogi nodded in affirmation.

"He killed him," Saif mumbled again in disbelief.

"You must leave town as soon as possible before Hatim comes looking for you" Nabeel had said to Yosef, who was now going in and out of consciousness. Days later, after being treated at a private clinic, Yosef had left for Shangrila.

Saif embraced Yosef with a hug under the willow tree.

"He talked about you till the day he died," Saif said.

"I remembered him too, while away," Yosef responded.

"Was he in pain when he left?"

"Jogi died in peace, *bhai*," Saif responded. "He died in his sleep. We found him in the morning in the Ring."

A cool breeze blew, causing leaves to rustle around them. Yosef felt goosebumps on his arms.

"Who has taken over?" Yosef asked.

"No one yet. We are meeting tonight at Café Pyala. I was hoping you could join us," Saif said.

"Not sure if I can stay that long," Yosef smiled.

"If we talk to Nabeel, then maybe …?"

"Maybe. But let's go say our final goodbyes to Jogi first."

They walked back toward the grave site. The *imam* made the final call for *janaza* (funeral prayer) and asked for lines to be formed. Yosef and Saif took up a position beside Nabeel.

"Feels good to be back," Yosef said in a lowered voice.

"I am glad you are here," Nabeel responded back.

"You never said what you did to make Hatim stop looking for me," Yosef said.

"What makes you think I did something?"

"He could have come looking for me in Shangrila if he wanted to. There wasn't much I could do to stop him."

"If he had known you were in Shangrila, then yes, he could have," Nabeel said.

"Hatim is standing right now at the gate, staring at us. Something is stopping him from coming over and dragging me away." Nabeel saw Hatim half hidden behind the entrance gate, intently gazing at Yosef

The *imam*, standing next to Jogi's shrouded corpse, raised his hands to his ears and said out loud, "*Allahu Akbar* (Allah is great)." The worshippers behind him followed suit. A few rows back, Nabeel put a finger on his lips, motioning Yosef to be quiet and follow the *imam*'s lead.

The air echoed with his charismatic voice as the *imam* recited:

"O Allah! grant forgiveness to our living and to our dead, and to those who are present and to those who are absent, and to our young and our old folk, and to our males and females. O Allah! whosoever you grant to live from among us, help him to live in Islam, and whosoever of us you cause to die, help him to die in faith. O Allah! do not deprive us of the reward for patience on his loss, and do not make us subject to trail after him."

The grave diggers moved in after the prayer to lower the body into the grave. The *imam* approached Nabeel and Yosef and asked if the deceased had the eldest male in the family present to supervise the burial.

"We are as close to a family Jogi had," Saif said.

"Jogi was an orphan. His family was killed in Afghanistan before he came to Pakistan," Nabeel explained to the *imam*, who shook his head in dismay.

"With your permission, I would like to supervise the burial," Yosef stepped up and said. "He was like a brother to me." The image of Jogi dangling from the overhanging wooden porch, rescuing him and Daud from Meera on their first day in Lahore ran through Yosef's eyes.

They watched Jogi's wrapped body being laid into the grave without a coffin, and took turns circling the grave each pouring three handsful of dirt into it.

"We created you from it, and return you into it, and from it we will raise you a second time," they chanted.

The cool shadows of the evening had become larger by the time they left the cemetery. One last time the grave diggers watered the unmarked grave where Jogi was buried. Slow burning cedar incense turned into ashes. In Jogi's remembrance, they shared stories about him. They laughed at jokes Jogi used to tell. They marveled how an orphan from Afghanistan had kept them together. There were some who kept their heads down and remembered how Jogi had dragged them out of the slums where they begged and took drugs.

They remembered Jogi as a friend, a brother, a leader.

Yosef, Nabeel, and Saif walked slowly behind rest of the gang. Saif hummed:

On the mountain's slope

The assembled trees form a dark green mass.

The stars twinkle,

And the moonlight adorns the Valley ....

"You never answered my question," Yosef said to Nabeel.

"Did you see Hatim there on your way out?"

"No, he disappeared," Yosef said.

"Let's just say I have enough dirt on him to expose him and put him behind bars."

"Does he know that?"

"He knows if he ever comes near you he will be on the front page of the next morning's paper."

Yosef's brows arched. He gave Nabeel an inquisitive look.

"It means you are welcome to move back to Lahore anytime you like." Nabeel patted Yosef's back and smiled.

They heard a commotion up ahead and noticed the crowd dispersing.

"What is going on?" Nabeel asked.

"It's the new kid," Saif mumbled, looking ahead. "I just saw him stealing fruit from the fruit vendor's cart. Now the merchant is chasing him down."

"Newbie, ugh!" Yosef grunted.

They heard the sound of a shrill whistle blowing and heavy footsteps rushing their way.

"Here we go," Yosef smiled.

"Police!" someone in the crowd yelled. "Run!"

And they ran, in every direction, like an enraged river gushing through a broken dam. They were the children of the streets. They knew the corners, the turns, the secret openings. And the beaten-down paths and cobblestone streets welcomed them with open arm, like mothers welcoming their children back home. After all, they hugged the streets back every night they slept, only to wake up and survive another day.

ABOUT THIS BOOK

This novel is based on a true story.

Over a period of six months, as reported by the New York Times, BBC, and other media outlets, in 1999, a serial killer named Javed Iqbal enticed street children to his apartment in Lahore with the promise of food and friendship. Once a child was weak and vulnerable, Iqbal would suffocate them with cyanide and dissolve their bodies in a vat of acid and dump the liquid paste into a local sewer. He kept a detailed journal of each murder, including the cost. He also took photographs of each victim and saved their clothing and personal effects, in order to prove what he had done.

Iqbal turned himself in to the Pakistani authorities after reaching his goal of one hundred children.

On March 16, 2000, the court in Lahore, Pakistan, sentenced Iqbal to be hanged in front of the families of his victims and to be cut into 100 pieces, which would be dissolved in acid. A few months after the decree, pending appeal to his sentence Javed Iqbal was found dead in his prison cell, strangled by the bed sheet on the bench he slept on.

This book is dedicated to the victims of Javed Iqbal's heinous crimes, whose voices vanished with their souls.

ABOUT THE AUTHOR

For nearly twenty years before coming to America, Zia Ahmad lived in the historic city of where this story takes place. He now resides in Chicago, and has a career in banking.

Connect on facebook:

http://www.facebook.com/onehundredthebook

Made in the USA
Charleston, SC
25 April 2012